PUBLISHER TURNED INTO A DOG

Gail Morgan is a writer, publisher and teacher of migrants. Her other works include the acclaimed novels *Promise of Rain* (Virago) and *Walk to Kulentufu* (Houghton Mifflin).

GAIL MORGAN
THE DAY MY PUBLISHER TURNED INTO A DOG

Illustrations by Nigel Buchanan

Frances Allen
Sydney

First published 1989
by Frances Allen
Sydney Australia

This paperback edition published 1990.

© Gail Morgan 1989

All rights reserved. No part of this publication may be reproduced, stored in a retrieval system, or transmitted in any form or by any means, electronic, mechanical, photocopying, recording or otherwise, without prior permission of the publisher.

National Library of Australia
Cataloguing-in-Publication entry:
Morgan, Gail, 1953– .
The day my publisher turned into a dog.
ISBN 0 947245 03 0.
I. Title.
A 823.3

Edited by Gillian Armitage
Illustrated by Nigel Buchanan
Designed in hardback by Robin James
Design adapted for paperback by John Ferrier
Typeset in 13½/16pt Bembo
by Solo Typesetting, South Australia
Printed in Australia on APM paper by
Australian Print Group
Promoted by Deborah Wood Publicity

To Margaret Connolly

My tale begins in Sydney town, that queasy little den of commerce balancing in dramatic arabesque on our eastern seaboard.

I tell the story of Jane Hardacre. Me. A piece of unpleasantness stuck to the corporate boot. She can't be found in the central business district, amidst the high-rise ruins of free enterprise. There are no good natured hucksters to welcome her as she comes through the plate glass door, employing that famous laconic wit which passes for cultural identity.

Hardacre has a story to tell which few will believe. It takes place in the suburbs, where the corporate shadow lengthens into a full corona.

Imagine yourself behind the peephole of a flat, my flat on Malabar Road, looking through the distorting glass to the world beyond. Double lock the door. You can stay inside. I have a story to tell which is well nigh fantastical. I will do my best to keep all shabby and threatening moments at bay. Let's have a laugh before shadows lengthen from city to sea. There isn't much time; there's no escaping things—for me at least.

We'll start by stretching credibility to the limit. I am

the sensationally beautiful Jane Hardacre. Every day, men approach me hushed and reverent, as if in a cathedral. Their suits are sweaty and crumpled, their hands shake like ageing monsignors on the brink of retirement, and their eyes are lit like votive candles beseeching me, Hardacre, for some sign of heavenly acquiescence.

My butcher sends me flowers. My florist sends me meat. The doctor begs for a phial of my phlegm. A petition was sent throughout the eastern suburbs to beg me not to leave them for Kirribilli. The other day a pest controller gassed himself under the flats when I refused to have a chat.

Rewind. Let's start again. I haven't quite told you the truth. I am not sensationally beautiful. In fact I am hideously ugly. I am so deformed it is hard to extract one monstrous feature from the other. A human pizza. Something scraped off a wall.

Last week the butcher mistook me for the mutton he'd ordered a month ago. He grabbed the cowl neck of my hand-knitted natural fibre jumper and cursed me for being late. I dare not enter the florist's, for it's the pelargoniums, not the pest man, that gas themselves as I enter.

Stop once again. Most people see themselves as extremes, and I suppose I'm no exception. The real truth is that I'm extraordinarily ordinary. God created the mouse so I could be compared to it. I am so nondescript, people crash into me in supermarkets, apologising to shelves full of feminine hygiene products. When I cross at a pedestrian crossing I have to walk alongside someone else, otherwise I'd be rally-crossed with tyre tread and indecipherable at the morgue.

All this is by-the-by. For I have a story to tell, and I will tell it with a tale wind in subtropical Sydney. City of pulsing blue sky, Byzantine harbour and enslaving sea. Here, life can transform. All is magic, falseness and sleight of hand. Yet it is an amateur performance, always on the brink of anarchy. Hold onto your tickets for the lucky door prize, and be damned sure to praise the performance on your way out.

My job is to tell something like the truth. I am, if you like, the noisy plumbing that rattles and clanks backstage. A writer. Moral tax collector. But my pariah status should not concern you. It is only relevant because of the story I have to tell.

Perhaps my progress will not be interesting. I am no rakish fop with semen on his satin breeches. Nor am I a muscle bound marketing manager measuring the inches of erect column on screen. That world is cynically optimistic. In that world there is bravado, and bravado is the fibreglass sarcophagus that entombs.

If you come with me you'll find there are surprises. I will ferry you across to a world of sentiment, and even if my way is false, you'll feel different at the end. No one has the answers, and you can use this accusation against me. But I ask you not to abandon Hardacre, for she, at least, means well; goes to sea in a leaky craft. You, dear reader, must supply her with safe harbour. For she is keen to recount her travels.

JANE HARDACRE lived in Epping, at the home of her parents—Valerie and Dan. Imagine her house, fifties log cabin with brick foundations. Lots of quick-growing eucalypts and fast-spinning spiders. In the fifties, nature boomed beside the babies. It made way for them. It fell into frozen tableaux around wooden playpens, and it helped to give three-dimensionality to sandpits, incinerators and mountains of rotting compost.

It was a burgeoning time, and Jane burgeoned. Her childhood was no more desperately miserable than anyone else's. She collected show bags, read erotic literature, joined the brownies but rebelled against the guides. She had a series of pets, all of whom died tragic, senseless, deaths—whose graves are now marked with river stones behind the barbeque.

Jane was a pretty child. One of those blonde angels that nowadays drape across supermarket trolleys. A real cliche with corkscrew curls and laughing eyes.

Pert and plentiful, she, and many others, were the pride of their age.

Things changed soon enough. The sixties brought acne and ironed hair. Her slim frame expanded like fold-out furniture, and she found she was taking after her father. It was then that Hardacre learned about transformation. Beauty and innocence vanished over night. Abandoned without explanation—frumpishness occasioned new responsibility. She had to become nice. This meant listening to the woes of the beautiful, and feeling superior to those who studied, or tried to please the teachers.

Messages of mediocrity were never lost on Jane. People, even beautiful people, needed reassurance. She learnt to scatter cliches like rosebuds in May, to cover her tracks in the primal corporation that was school. The miracle was that she failed, that even mediocrity was no guarantee. A certain malice was needed to ensure success, and in spite of her desperate need for popularity, Hardacre could not succumb to it. She passed her days in disbelief, that people could be so cruel and life so hard.

Whilst Jane remained suspended in her state of disbelief, life snuck by. For life in those days kept its counsel, had not become a fat overlord carried complaining on a creaking litter. In those days life did not proffer its blubbery bejewelled hand for her to admire. It was lean, and turned the pages of a secret diary.

Then, life struck quickly and without warning. Sometimes it took the form of a school concert that went horribly wrong. At other times she found herself 'dobbed in'.

The dobber is essential to the primal corporation that is school. She sniffs her nosegay of 'ersions' (subversion, perversion) that when taken to a teacher transform miraculously into 'ations' (recrimination, micturation, incarceration, with the inevitable invitation for parents to visit the school).

At boys' schools humiliation was more open and ran to the 'ing' words (ballocking, punching, drubbing, licking, jobbing, thumping, swearing, knifing — all allowable within the 'ing' *do* nasty of the male playground). There were times when Hardacre wanted to be a boy. Male power seemed infinite. But she knew that growing up was harder for men, that they lacked the courage to face the shrinking world of adulthood.

The highlight of High School for Jane was her final year. She shocked the starlets in Year 12 by scoring a hunk. 'Hunk' is a scholastic euphemism for examination failure. His closest living relative is 'the spunk' who, whilst not being as well built, still holds vast quantities of sex appeal.

Jane's hunk surfed. His hair was blonde breakers down his back. Furtive and close set were his escapee eyes, empty and unattainable was his demeanour. Jane and Dave would go on endless drives up the coast in his white VW, always with another couple. The men sat together in the front. Their combined weight would cause the nose of the beetle to dip, and like a vacuum cleaner it seemed to suction the very bitumen off the roads.

Jane would sit in the back with the other woman. There were times when they looked sheepish and seconded, unable to hear a word from the front seats. Often they were grateful for the chance for some feminine parley, discussing endlessly the problems of a bikini line and removing unwanted hair.

Hardacre had fair skin, so the beach was hell. Her epidermis did the dance of seven veils until she was covered with birthmarks, blotches and freckles. Unfit to face man or beast, her hair tangled like coastal casuarina. Dave's attachment to her became affectionate and sentimental, as though she were a mangy camp dog who had refused to go away.

This trial by burning strengthened Jane's love of the sea. Every weekend she would watch Dave bobbing like a cork on the waves. No message. No bottle. Just blonde and reassuring emptiness. But knowledge shadowed the horizon like a little black cloud—Jane was fascinated by its loutish energy as it skudded across the sea.

Back at school Hardacre discussed the latest surfing films with authority. There were times when it behoved her to wax lyrical. Her legs, his board. His libido which frightened them both. In short, she ended up in secretarial college.

This was the beginning of the end for Hardacre. Having consciously made the wrong decision, she felt she could now call herself 'grown up'. Secretarial college bled into her consciousness like a failed marriage. She began to construct diverse rescue fantasies, planning a brilliant divorce settlement, a rosy future that belied her inescapable poverty of circumstance.

Hardacre lashed herself to the mast of self recrimination. She had been lazy, indifferent. This was her reward. Mediocrity was the waratah in her crown. Nowadays the business of survival had to be taken seriously. It was cut-throat, when all she had was something blunt and plastic, a knife for a kid's birthday party.

Instead of perfecting her shorthand, she should join the band of young turks, cutting their teeth on business practice and the media. But she was no turk, which was the key as she saw it to her problems. A fierce and overweening scepticism ruled her. The prizes of the world looked increasingly shabby, like mangy objects on display at a fairground. When she was young she hadn't noticed fur missing on the tiger, or seen the wine stain on the kangaroo.

Hardacre began to blame life's inadequacies on herself. That seemed the adult thing to do. There were, moreover, lots more blind alleys to be tried.

Hardacre was still young enough to be seduced by the ambush. Hadn't she always wanted to be given a surprise party? The kind of hilarious gig they turned on in American movies.

To cut a long story short, Hardacre was a failure. Dry-docked in the typing pool of the Crown Solicitor's Department. Her job, pre-word processing, was to type up documents with their relevant amendments. There were summonses, notifications of intent to proceed ex-parte, egg levy audits, parking violations under the Airport Surface Traffic Act, the many sundry grievances associated with a federal-state tug of law.

The desks of fellow typists were close by. The office resembled both a Surry Hills sweat shop and a teenage pyjama party. Older women typed with crabbed claw hands. The younger ones had supple fingers like pianists with long fingernails.

Hardacre felt out of place, condemned, metaphysically speaking, to wearing outsized boots around the office. People made way for her, expecting her to knock things over. They looked at her curiously, especially when she produced Gibbon's 'Decline and Fall' to read over lunch breaks. Every day she grew an inch taller, or so it seemed, as she hunched self consciously over documents. The Hardacre incubus became, like the law itself, ungovernable.

The typing pool spilled over into an ocean of discontent. Workers focused their grievances on lawyers, languishing in their own offices upstairs, never giving a second thought to the slaves below. Lawyers were tasteless, wore brown suits (in those days they were all men), couldn't spell, were ridiculously overpaid, never learnt anyone's name, yoked grammatical clauses together like asthmatic oxen to pull a negligible burden of meaning. Lawyers distrusted punctuation. A comma undermined the solidity of any relationship. It was a faltering, an ambiguity that made them think of the outside world.

Nevertheless Hardacre, like others in the oppressed classes, held half-hearted hopes of landing a marlin in a three-piece. A young up-and-coming whose father was a judge. A smart pup with killer eyes. The sort who used government service in the Crown as a stepping stone, who held bureaucracy in amused contempt whilst extracting absurd travelling allowances from a hostile pay section. She knew her marlin. But did he know her?

Not likely. No lawyer would have a bar of, let alone enter 'the bar' with, Hardacre from the typing pool—

encircling his arm like a band of funereal mourning. She had all the charm of a divorcee without a property settlement. Her personality was dull enough for a lawyer, but the problem was her poverty, powerlessness and impatience.

There was no choice. She knew with the certainty of statute that she would have to change jobs. Otherwise, no marlin. A job out there was prompting her. An alter ego was waiting in the wings. She was, she felt, more gatherer than hunter. In an interesting, dispassionate sort of occupation, she could pick up the pieces after her marlin's first defeat in court. But she needed the right persona. Any persona. A job that rendered her visible.

Jane chose advertising. This was an industry where the ugly and insecure could dominate the 'beautiful people'. The idea appealed. Any unworthiness of motive could be counter-balanced by generous gratuities to Val and Dan. Typing was so badly paid.

Hardacre imagined herself in that Valhalla which was, for the purposes of reverie, North Sydney. She saw herself sitting in some inter-galactic office tower, eyes twin lasers assessing the suitability of some muscle-bound puck, dressed down to his socks. 'No. I'm afraid you won't do. We want a marlin in a three-piece.' Fantasy would come easy on the fiftieth floor of a cathode tube tower. She could look down on that intricate map of Sydney and chart her course. When people came into her office, she wouldn't have to speak. Electrical impulses would fire from her brain as invisible sunshowers. She would watch her messages encoded by other workers, defective egotistical machines who, in spite of an early appointment at the gym, would do her bidding.

Hardacre saw herself surrounded by chic screwballs in mini-mokes, handsome men in pale linen suits, aspiring writers, failed writers, quirky intellectuals, pretenders, innocents with every known sexually transmittable disease, cynics with two marriages and custody on weekends.

Cognisant of human frailty, Hardacre would simply bide her time grovelling on her belly to certain clients, until she rose like Venus out of her conch, taking as many valuable customers as possible, to open her own Grotto of Capri at McMahons Point.

THAT WAS THE PLAN. So Jane proceeded from tower to tower, interview to interview, until she thought warm days would never cease. Young, resilient, rejection rarely worried her — in fact it strengthened her resolve. At least that was what she told herself, and

Val and Dan who rang after each interview.

There was, Jane felt, a certain macabre interest that went with explaining oneself. She was flattered even by an interviewer's feigned concern. Young and unsure, she assumed the air of the debutante 'coming out' in the world.

Humiliations were many and jobs were few. Hardacre had plenty of time to ponder the human condition, but desperation and debt drove her into a state of mindless reverie—all her attention went into keeping the human condition at arm's length.

Why hadn't she done better at school? Why didn't she have long brown legs and perfect teeth? She was as ordinary as all stations to Lidcombe. Her cv read like the minutes of a short body corporate meeting.

Was there any hope at all for the battler from Epping? No. Not in advertising. Her final prospect bit the metaphorical dust when her shoe caught in the coaster of a chair. You, dear reader, know the kind I mean—a predatory Danish octopus with exclusive fishing rights in North Sydney office blocks. She'd tried to make the most of things by getting down on her hands and knees and swearing at it, showing she was no wimpish airline steward who'd pretend the whole thing hadn't happened. But plastic shoes had made her feet sweat, and the accounts executive had drawn back in distaste. Had she had the money to buy Italian, the whole thing might never have happened.

She began to brood. Perhaps she owned one of those lives whose coasters were destined to jam. To dignify it with the description 'bad luck' was going too far. She had had her share of good times. But she began to wonder why things rarely worked to plan. A plan, she felt, was like a curse on those who'd lost their innocence. A decision to go into advertising was solid gold security that she would never end up in the industry. Perhaps she would be better off compiling a list of things she didn't want to do, to ensure they would never happen. Or was such a double whammy worth the risk?

Jane decided to go for other kinds of jobs. She put on her interview suit for a further six months, her wet suit wherein she made mouths at the fish, sharks, and all those different species in employment. Her air supply often felt endangered. Occasionally she would stoop so low she would suffer from the bends when she got home. Landing a marlin in a three-piece was looking more and more difficult. She began to mourn for the fish that got away. Perhaps she should ring him up, ask for legal advice, suggest they discuss the problem over dinner at her flat. The chief problem was her flat. It had all the exuberance of Trotsky's grave, ex-Housing Commission on Malabar Road. One neighbour was a strong unionist, the other swore by the new right. There were duels in the corridor over car spaces, bird droppings, rubbish disposal, and use of the laundry. The unionist went round in a dressing gown all day, while the facist wore his polyester jumpsuit and running shoes. The place was like a bad dream, except it was difficult to dream on Malabar Road when so little sleep could be had.

Her candlelight dinner would have all the charisma of an evening at the abattoirs. The marlin, no doubt, would want to talk about himself, and she would discreetly juggle the hotplates, or rather hotplate, of her stove. He would have to shout into the kitchen: 'I've been with Attorney General's now for five years, and I've been thinking of a) going to the bar, or b) hanging up my shingle.' And she would have to sound enthusiastic with fat hissing and crackling, poppadums turning up their toes like dissatisfied criminal clients. 'Really?' she would say as her marlin leapt into view, 'I'll be all right here. Don't worry. What does going to the bar entail?' The marlin would reel back on his finny haunches. 'Briefly, briefs.' And then they would both laugh as the hook flirted with his mizzen fin. And there would be a brief time of warmth until the plates arrived like loaded carts of night soil. His mouth would drop with distaste. Her marlin would be used to nouvelle cuisine, his vegies dressed, fanned and dainty as southern belles. She would have to flatter the pants off him to compensate. And if he didn't drink, the night would be a total failure. What was the use? Hardacre had none of the hostess skills that went with geishadom in the West. Her marlin would swim away with relief, out to sea and into the nets of some bigger trawler.

Jane Hardacre reluctantly took stock of herself. Still unemployed, now so afraid of mirrors she dressed by the reflection of a window. There was a definite image problem somewhere. The world, she felt, had to deal in stereotypes, for these were the only real security in people's lives. Like children, they let you down, but at the same time guaranteed a false immortality, a sense of generational continuity. Hardacre dwelt on her own stereotype, the one that linked her with all the dowdy women of history, padding after successful husbands in blue stockinged feet.

In desperation she turned to women's magazines. Like the political pamphlets of yesteryear, they sought to enlighten. She devoured them like amphetamines, racing from one article to the next, borne along with the masses in a state of self loathing and restless discontent. 'Why am I not rich and famous?' 'Why aren't I slim enough to fit through the eye of a needle?' 'Who are these people sending in their handy hints?' 'What church-going goody-two-shoes knows that mustard gets out stains when heated to a temperature of 2000 degrees celsius?'

After a few weeks with the rich and glamorous, her life lay ahead of her like a five year plan—boring, optimistic, and totally unconvincing.

Hardacre needed advice, and she needed it quickly. She couldn't go to Val and Dan. They were already helping her pay the rent, and had worries of their own. There had to be someone objective, dispassionate, nearby, who could scribble out a prescription for the future.

After some desperate and hasty deliberation, the unionist from next door came to mind. He had always seemed authoritative in his floor length robes. Oracular. There'd been a time when this man had had the ear of many famous people, but bluntness and inability to compromise had been his undoing.

'There is something about you,' he said, removing the tray from his budgie cage, 'that reminds me of myself in my heyday.' He looked at the bird. 'Or perhaps you're more like Jack.'

'More like Jack?'

'After his industrial accident.'

'Oh.'

'When he became a writer. You should become a writer.'

'But I've got nothing to say.'

'All the better.' He filled the water trough. 'They'll love you.'

'What would I write?'

'Romances,' he sniffled. The backs of his slippers had entirely collapsed. 'Or detective yarns, like Jack.'

'It all sounds too easy.'

'I think you'll write better than him.'

'Why?'

'You're the perfect insecure little bourgeois, and you haven't got arthritis.'

'I'll work hard,' she added enthusiastically.

'Not too hard.' His voice went flat. 'No typing after nine, what with the aircraft I couldn't stand it.'

Hardacre left her neighbour. She was transformed.

At last she had a raison d'etre. Self respect opened like a flower in her soul. Just one step down from a journalist. Typing for herself from now on, not others. She began to feel independent, proud. Just one step down from a journo. When journalists wanted to self destruct, they became writers. Perhaps she could rise from the ashes of literature one day to become a journalist. It was her dream at least. She needed social approval as much as the next person.

Hardacre decided to write sagas. These were cosy, family, bosomy things, and they would welcome the apprentice. Sagas suited her plodding temperament, her typing skills, her youthful lack of knowledge and library research capacity.

It never occurred to Hardacre to bare her soul. The loneliness inside her all tangled and twisted like barbed wire would, she felt, be of little interest to the reader. Even if she could untangle the wire and explain herself, it would still be there, fencing her in and someone else out.

Sagas would do her fine. They'd make her money, friends, and they would free her from Malabar Road. One day she'd wake up and find herself confident, like a woman recovering from amnesia. A kind marlin would be stooping over her as she fought to remember that other time when she'd been awkward and lonely.

This, dear reader, is how Hardacre transformed. Her craft a fairy godmother, its price, hard work. She would slave as a waitress to subsidise her fairy queen, serving haddock to business marlen, telling them haughtily she was a writer and not interested in anything but a good night's sleep.

So in spite of innate insecurity, Hardacre began the long, disciplined march towards the bestseller. Stubbornness would keep her on the straight and narrow, enthusiasm prodding her from behind like a sadistic scout leader. She would produce ten pages a day, and one book a year. The Hardacre juggernaut had begun.

IT IS PECULIAR how life looks so unfavourably on juggernauts. Determination, whilst being the most admired of virtues, is often the least valued. This is probably because it implies failure. Once success has been achieved, determination can be abandoned like a dowdy spouse. In a swiftly dying world, this virtue can appear as luxury and delusion. It costs too much time, points to waste. Hardacre had little concept of how ill-judged determination could be.

She wrote five sagas for Forget-Me-Not Press, before one was accepted. It was the first she'd written for them, under a different title. Hardacre retitled and rewrote the other four, and what with valuable editorial suggestions, true mediocrity was achieved.

Her sagas were insipid things, lengthy testaments to the Australian squattocracy. Most of the background came from obscure provincial newspapers. There were accounts of fox hunting and polo, picnic races and balls. Women with English complexions picked their way across the social pages, trying to avoid horse dung. Men stood round trestle tables complimenting fierce matrons on the punch. It was another world, and it held Hardacre in amused contempt. In this world, desirable women in jodhpurs performed their dressage, and handsome judges awarded ribbons to the prettiest sitting trot. Cut glass whisky decanters rested on oak bureaux, while pert daughters of prominent graziers rebelled.

Hardacre began to see life as meaningless. Slowly she was being sucked into a void. Every day she lost particles of awareness, confidence. It seemed God was filing her down, and the publishing industry had become His emery board.

'Forget-Me-Not Press' was the piquant name given to the subsidiary of the huge multi-national that published Hardacre sagas. In Jane's mind it was something offshore, floating unclaimed, like nuclear waste no one will own up to.

The editor was Rowena, the publisher, Delphine. Both women were paragons of their sex, and with two paragons in the one building it would have been hard for an author to cut a dash.

These paragons of beauty and accomplishment held Hardacre in contempt. They would glare both barrels at her as she entered the office, and Hardacre would feel embarrassed, obsequious, as if she were trying to sell them something past its prime, a common or garden hare that had hung too long on the back porch.

It was, she felt, her fault the Australian market was so small. Both Rowena and Delphine wanted to be in New York, where blockbusters took like petrol on a vacant warehouse. The home product was a sad affair, a little puppy trailing after an older dog in its prime. Neither Delphine nor Rowena dared push the Australian product overseas. They were not going to insult the world with an idiot child.

So writing sagas did not prove remunerative for Hardacre. If her income soared into the thirty per cent tax bracket she was thrilled, felt like throwing a barmizvah. In a small country, Hardacre felt, they wouldn't let you sell anything—not even your soul.

The reality of being small, an out-of-towner, sharpened Jane's resolve. She would just have to write better books. That way she'd please herself as well as everyone else. Everyone but Delphine. Moreover life wasn't that bad in Malabar Road. In a hot climate one didn't need the sun. She'd grown used to the traffic noise, in fact it helped her write.

What if she tried to tell the truth about herself? Life? After five sagas, she was entitled to be foolhardy. It felt like rebellion. Or rather, she was going on strike. No more graziers, no more love trysts behind the shearers' huts. Hers would be a moral strike in order to achieve lower pay. She knew this was un-Australian. But how would she know what this really meant until she wrote about it?

When it came down to it, Hardacre wanted to use her brain. She craved the poor person's aphrodisiac 'self respect'. She had the flat shoes to go with it. There was enough self pity in her to feed an army of starving orphans.

She would become Jane Hardacre—serious writer, whose glum and inauspicious words would suit the maiden speech of an undertaker at his first triennial embalming conference.

Pause button. She was not all that serious. She was merely vulnerable, and she would make herself more vulnerable in that constant act of self annihilation which was the written word.

Would Delphine give her a handicapped sticker for her car? Or would the demon jaws (honed on diet crackers and late afternoon crayfish lunches) of vulpine Delphine devour her. Delph could take full advantage of a 'serious writer'. She could sniff out weakness like an anorexic tracker dog on its first hunt. There would be no kindliness from Delphine.

You, dear reader, will hear a lot more about Delphine. Delph is not the liberated woman, she's the super woman. In fact she's been genetically engineered. The super woman, like the super sheep, cow, or tomato is large, delicious, and shows no disfiguring marks. She is for display, and has a long corporate shelf life. Woe betide the person who seeks sustenance from her.

Unsuccessful writers, felt Hardacre, were blemishes on the industry, like wheat rust or weevil. They were the sediment in the Margaux, the grit in the oyster, the filigree line of black on the back of the prawn. Hardacres were liabilities, and from a social point of view, were as dull as open drains in a drought.

Woe is me moaned Jane, daughter of Valerie and Dan. Many's the time I've observed Delph's late lunches. Many's the time I've watched her offsiders heaping books onto the fire or the book pulping truck. For many are the failures and irascible is the great god bestseller. I have seen this deity extract huge advances, only to allow the book to sell below its projected millions. Life is cruel. So revenge must be taken on the little people, the mildly successful, first novelists, serious novelists, anyone who breaks just a little above even. These are the worker bees who must subsidise an over-promoted queen.

This my dear readers is commerce, and I make no excuses for it. Waste and profligacy are its hallmarks, indifference is the result. I speak of commerce conducted on behalf of someone else. Corporate life with its corporate class pets. I speak of the righteousness of monopolies, and of the brutish basilicas built by foreign powers, inhabited by the talentless effigies of other men's gods.

'This is my industry,' thought Hardacre. 'Do I dare write something worthwhile?'

She put herself in the foyer of the Lewisham office, trying to imagine Delphine's reaction: 'This concept is too refined, that, too threadbare. I find your characters too, I don't know, shabby. But you can always re-write, can't you? I do think though, that if you used 'do' as much as I do, you'd do much better, don't you think?'

Hardacre allowed a spasm of a smile to animate her plain face. It was all so hopeless. There was a certain challenge to setting one's sights lower and lower, bargaining down into negative figures, disappearing into transcendental nothingness like a Buddhist fasting throughout the year.

Jane put herself in Delphine's office: 'Just remember Jane, our business is business, yours is writing. We blindfold our writers for their own protection. Writers aren't interested in print runs, production details, marketing, the jacket of their book. Why should they be interested? They wrote the book, and that's enough work for one person. We are, after all, putting up the money (I'm careful not to say "making" in this situation). We are investing an amount equal to the average addition, home renovation, to a suburban bungalow in Sydney's outer west. Yes, I mean a top storey. A top storey for a top story. You should be grateful.'

Grateful to whom? To Forget-Me-Not? The corporation that has never read any of its own books. To Forget-Me-Not, a small imprint swept up into the vortex of an international money market where books and bidets, literature and mood lighting inhabit the same bed?

The quaint little terrace in Lewisham was a sham. Or perhaps it was wisely chosen. It made one think of a lower middle class household in nineteenth century England. The 'kitchen maids' who held full time positions were, in their capacities as publisher and editor, able to admonish the odd job people—scullery maids and writers—whose seasonal work was both gruelling and poorly paid. This quaint little terrace in Lewisham was a perfect reflection of an undercapitalised industry inherited from the tightwad English upper classes.

Rowena is the editor of Forget-Me-Not. She is young, pretty, and extremely highly strung. Her good looks allow her to be officious and humourless in turns. She has a well punctuated face, with lots of 'do's and conformities. Her smile is her Achilles heel. It stalls like a racehorse at the gate. There is a nerve-racking ruthlessness which shows up in her grooming. Her casualness is arranged like the perfect crime. Custodian of the image, she possesses the guarded air of a school prefect hiding amorality.

Rowena knows everybody. She gushes over them like a garden hose with an ill-adjusted nozzle. She is on familiar terms with every publisher, journalist, editor, promotions person. At a restaurant she's as reliable as Reuters, relaying snippets about the impecunious and the important.

Rowena's problem is simply that she spent too long in England working as a lowly sub-editor. Her social climbing skills went to waste in Australia. The industry here had no social prestige. It was a poor relation, and as tainted as the clergy.

Delphine was well aware of image problems. This was why she aligned herself with the US. Delphine did her best to take authors and books out of the industry.

Her business was to launder money, and remit profits overseas. It was only in private that she could boast about being a patron of the arts.

There had been a lot of patronising, observed Hardacre, over the years. Both Rowena and Delphine were used to talking in hushed and reverant tones about 'successful authors'. For the most part these prodigies lived overseas. Each success story was a lash of reproach to the mildly profitable, like Jane. Had she lost money on one of her books, treated her editor shabbily, maligned fellow authors, she might at least have been feared. But as it was, she was that least desirable of commodities, ballast. Hardacre was the muzak that played in the lift heading for the bestselling penthouse.

Ballast? Ballardist? Which would she be, now that the worm had turned. 'Let me drag them across the hot coals of holy words and let me pluck off their unholy beards. My priestly mantle of cliche and surplus of collocation must drop to the ground. Let everyone praise the Lord it is not they who have been called to serve the pen.'

If only she wasn't so slab-like. 'I'm an antipodean Stonehenge. I don't give a toss that I don't belong, that I stand out like a sore thumb and measure time against the horizon. For I am no patriot, no under-age adolescent drinking at the pub to prove his manhood. If they want my exuberance to be drunken and false, then I'll refuse to exube.

'Let everyone praise the Lord it is not they who have been called to serve the pen,' Hardacre repeated. The words held the illusion of being spoken. 'There by the grace of me, go they. I wonder if they know the cruel fate that, actuarially speaking, I am saving them from.'

Hardacre imagined hard-hearted Rowena shedding a virgin tear for struggling writers. The same hard heart flaking off at the edges, like fingernail to the four winds. A remorseful Weenie would take up Hardacre's cause with Delphine. Publisher. El presidente in her corporate shades, lolling behind a pile of boardroom ryvitas, wearing designer suits, Italian (non-octopii-engaging) shoes and faultlessly unhairy hair.

This same Rowena might place the pathetic typescript at the feet of the Delphic oracle. And Delph would say: 'A serious novel? From Hardacre? You can't be serious.' But a flirtatious flutter would enter her voice. She can see the challenge that lies ahead. Feel the excitement of spending the barest minimum on a product, in order to watch a forgiving public chipping its way through the great wall of silence. It would make the world seem such an industrious, deserving sort of place.

'I fear I'm an incurable optimist,' sighed Hardacre, 'wanting to be a serious novelist, to share with readers the absurd mateship of "trying to understand". No one has wanted to share in the past. But I suppose when one is lonely one talks to oneself, hoping the typewriter will drown out the noise, render emotions comprehensible.'

Hardacre began to doubt the process of transformation. It is too miraculous, she felt, words carrying feelings, lodging like Cupid's arrows in the reader's heart. Nevertheless, I am prepared to shatter myself into a thousand pieces, on the offchance I re-assemble as a cathedral window. I will do my best to make the thing work, trying not to catch my own plain reflection in the design, or get a glimpse of the dizzying distance to life below. The world below is a dizzying place, spinning on its distaff, telling Falstaffian yarns, finding refuge in childish acts of subterfuge and spite.

Never had kind Valerie and Dan been more at its mercy, now that the years were rushing by at Liverpool. Every month Hardacre attended an orgy of ordinariness at Excalibur Retirement Village.

Her parents were living out their retirement in a state of siege. There was the constant roar of the traffic, the occasional thunderous slide of a semitrailer, cars in a barbed wire knot on the footpath. They played the genteel middle class, clinking their teacups, while the rabble roared in the streets. They dwelt on life in Australia before it became international and fast. At any moment they might be called on to die. A semi had claimed the life of Ivy Miller in the next room. Every time there was a collision they took stock of themselves, counted themselves lucky.

Hardacre reviewed her own barren life, a claypan for the serious novelist to turn over. At school she'd been as mediocre as banana custard. She'd graduated to a typing pool to be lowered down in a bamboo cage with the other lepers. There, she'd missed out on her marlin, finally deciding in her ad hoc fashion to become a writer. Such a past couldn't be dignified with the word 'failure'. Such a life had all the glamour of a knitting pattern. She was surviving its awfulness by searching for self respect—hand-knitted, out-of-shape self respect.

Hardacre, knowing she was an embarrassment, could not decide to whom: 'When I enter a room I choke on the tomb dust of pity. For I will be a serious novelist. The bearer of bad news. The personification of paltry hopes and feeble fantasies. When you need a cold shower come to me. For I pride myself on my self respect, that overpriced and out-of-shape thing one generation hands down to the next. An ugly heirloom that people refuse to throw away, get sentimental over then throw back into the attic with an "Uggh I just can't wear her".'

But, dear reader, remember the labour. It is not often these days you get something for nothing. Hardacre imagined Rowena taking the hat round the office to collect for the serious novelist. Warning the marketing people that everything possible was being done for the poor writer, and that they needn't worry about pushing her too hard. 'Just leave her to us in editorial,' she says. 'We will turn the manuscript into something worthwhile—not just worthwhile, something well punctuated and full of "do"s.' Rowena is a touch literal and something of a do-gooder. 'You marketing people leave our poor author alone. The last thing she needs is to be handled by the grimy denizens of commerce. There are dangers in over exposure. Leave her to us.'

   Then Delphine would emerge from the conference room having just spoken with someone famous, someone who possesses the wit of Erasmus, the humour of a New York cabbie, the iconoclasm of Swift. Delph would emerge swathed in the *swich licuor* of success, smiling triumphantly at her serious writer. 'Can you mix a good cocktail dear?' she might ask playfully. 'Of course we don't expect our serious authors to know their cocktails. Your metier is prose. Your atelier, the world. The fate of the human soul is in your hands. Don't treat this trust lightly, my yeoman of the soul. If it is only the Hardacres of the world who'll take the task seriously, then we must settle on the Hardacres of the world. You, my dear Jane, are where you are because no one else chooses to be where you are. Anyone can write a novel these days, what with word processors and the like. But few, I admit, possess the necessary quantities of self respect.'

She imagined herself shrinking with the shame of having chosen to enlighten. Vanity? Or self respect? If she worked hard the real issues might sink under the weight of her travails. Nevertheless it was a terrifying prospect this game of arbiter 'with hands tied'. Morally speaking it was like choosing to be an honest cop. She had flat feet, and the best years of her life to offer. But where was the romance?

Vanity? Or self respect? The critics would blur the distinction even further, having copious doubts of their own. They were the psychiatrists of the literary world. Not all. Some were experts in the forensic sciences, looking for traces of 'saga' in a serious novelist. Some could no doubt sniff out a dictaphone at fifty paces. The same people, so kind to the unemployed and socially disadvantaged, would see the serious novelist as gross presumption. They would smell the sweat of her aspirations, see her struggling out of her chair to brush her teeth, typing with her toes and missing the commode. If only her disadvantages had sprung from real illness instead of the need to write. The smaller she was, and the less she earned, the greater would be their indignation at a wasted life. Critics, concluded Hardacre, should wait until the author dies before they turn crown witness. Otherwise, opening fetes and handing out laurels would better occupy their time.

'I don't think I can write a good book,' Hardacre sighed. 'The one I want to write.' She shook her head.

'Shall I speak of setting suns in parallel universes, where there is gold for those who cross over? Shall I portray love and vain striving, ambition and betrayal? What if I surround my Delph in love, will she gurgle like a babe in a crib, weep tears of pity, or fail to see my typescript on her desk.'

Hardacre walked past imaginary cameras, arm in arm with Delphine. They winked at the judging panel. 'I've been supporting my authors for years,' says Delph. Then Delph would disengage her arm. 'We're partners. Her prose is so. . . . Well I do suggest you read it. Read it all my dears. Right away.' And she would present Hardacre with a crowning cocktail, flown in for the occasion from Barbados with a delicately thatched cap and three chimneys made from the skins of limes.

If she became an auteur with hauteur, one day she might land a marlin. But she suspected that marlen were for Marlenes, sexy deep-throated things that held down well paid jobs. Marlenes could find a boardroom in an office tower without having to ask directions. They lounged on banana chairs on private Pittwater beaches. They looked out onto their neighbour's success totally without rancour, to that pretty little Chinese junk with its silk sails purchased with last year's tax rebate. Their bars were low key, yet fully stocked. Fruity and barely alcoholic were drinks laced with success. No sweet sherry for them. Hardacre thought she could see her marlin swimming further and further out to sea. Her destiny was elsewhere.

But where else? Working nights and writing days was nobody's idea of fulfillment. Her name for a start was all wrong. Tolstoy (pronounced with Slavic grit), sounded like 'tall story' and thus invited the reader to read. Joyce could expound on the 'joys' of being himself. Kafka had the best name of all—cross between rug trader and prince of the desert. There he was in her imagination, morose and punctilious, caught up in the curtains of some splendid mansion, apologising aggressively for intruding, part poacher, part priest, withdrawing with martyred yet timely grace to continue his clerical libations behind teller bars. A name like 'Hardacre' conjured nothing but toil. It might as well be Jane 'Sweatboil'. Her name had all the glamour of a truss, suggesting overexertion and unwise ambition. Jane Hernia acre, daughter of Dan who wears a truss. She shows so little trust.

As for Delphine, oily and oracular, her name was perfect. Teacher's pet in the book trade. She'd commissioned a biography once whose subject had gone on to become prime minister. That success painted out her many failures. Besides, Forget-Me-Not was, as we already know, part of a huge conglomerate, possessing a large number of sinister Shiva hands. The concept of left and right had become obsolete, so too had the various products they produced. Delphine was certainly not out to make money, that might draw attention to herself, encourage corporate restructuring. Delph's object, like that of her male counterparts, was to remain invisible. A corporate effigy in designer suits. A dab hand at daiquiris. A patron of the arts—provided the arts were arts gratis arts. A reader of second rung literary novels luridly naturalistic and as homey as a chinwag with pals.

In fact I dream of you Delph in your camp commandant suits, seamed stockings as straight as a nazi salute. What do you find time to dream about? Little girls in lingerie? Or do you dream a grovel game with your marlin. Tell me, my svelte, as uncommunicative as a Sydney rock oyster. You play the corporate game with the composure of a hit man. Inedible above the tideline. I feel some vulgarity tart on your tongue. I slip on a patch of your profanity. Are cliches really 'mankind's only piece of common ground'? I wrote sagas for you until you thought warm days would never cease, but it's my turn now, Oh Delphine prettier than Rowene. You are the princess and I am the pea. I see your desk quite uncharted and free. The vase of flowers, that paperweight all alone from a satisfied author. I see a pile of manuscripts next to your desk, stacked on the floor like mattresses.

I await your husky voice Delph telling me about good books. For as you say, they promote themselves, and readers are quite psychic when faced with rows of good books. Most readers have a branch of willow in their heads which quivers uncontrollably at the first hint of watery treasure. They can find a philosopher's stone amidst the bedrock, being pleased to invest base metal at the till. 'Good books don't make money' you say. Not for their authors. Successive generations read the good books that don't make money for their authors. Furthermore Delph of my dreams, a good book depends on being well edited, and there is nothing better than a twenty year old for this enterprise. Nothing like the objectivity of a new generation in these matters. The test of time, so soon. And finally darling Delph, my sarcasm is wearing me down. I beg that when I finish my masterpiece you'll not send it out to too many readers, before you reject it.

So HARDACRE BEGAN her epic, evicting her illusions as callously as a landlord non-paying tenants. Her butt burgeoned. Her eyesight grew dim. Her feet held as flat and true as a carpenter's plane. In short, years went by.

During this time her typewriter tapping was prolific, but not quite as graceful as Astaire's. It was noted however that her typing could be heard down a stairwell or two. Three pages a day, until at the end of five years she'd amassed 5475 pages, 5000 of which were no good at all. Writing was no different from the insect world. It throve on waste. Indeed, God made the world that way so the few survivors could feel like millionaires if they chose.

Hardacre placed her survivors into their cicada shoebox. Characters who'd had to shout over the clatter of a typewriter to make themselves heard. Insecure siblings in a large family. Delph was their after life, the one instinctively they hadn't trusted. She would, no doubt, scald them with the everlasting fire of her coffee, laugh at their little despairs, shudder at a deformed image like a school teacher who hears the chalk squeak. In the end she might give a pretty sigh of disappointment, a good read being so hard to come by these days, and authors so helpless in their hubris. Her best move would be to hand the whole catastrophe over to a designer who, ho hum, would do the best she could with tiresome and tatty words.

Going to a publisher was like waiting to hear a will read. Benefits usually went elsewhere, and a smile of friendly indifference was the order of the day. Hardacre approached the Lewisham office with apprehension. I ask you dear reader to imagine a renovated

terrace next to a shabby warehouse—the concept of 'poor relation' in this way built into the bricks and mortar. Hardacre was very much the shabby door to door person. Her manuscript was dog eared, her shoes were so down at heel they resembled slippers. 'All I need now is an industrial accident,' she thought. 'It might help the finances for a while. No doubt they have smelt my desperation from as far away as Glebe Fish Markets.'

Hardacre had fallen on hard times, as most of us do. Being a serious novelist was looking less novel and more serious by the minute. Her waitressing wasn't enough to live on. Her capital was gone. No doubt she'd be offered some piddling advance by Delph. Damn writing to hell. Damn Delphine to hell, too. The woman might be underpaid by corporate standards, but she had a car, credit cards, two marlen, her own townhouse with electric garage door, intercom, swimming pool. Delph lived like a rosella in a gilded cage. At weekends she and Rowena would float on their lilos in the water tank, nibbling on their dietitious whole grain assiduously, parroting whatever accepted wisdom waggled its finger through their cage. It was all too much. Hardacre's imagination began to grow feverish.

Inside her manuscript box was a palpitating heart. Gross, red, revealing. People would one day gather round her book like it was a road accident. 'Oh my God, the poor woman. Where's her marlin? Uggh, there's something revolting there. Ugly and palpitating. Is it alive? It can't be true. Got to get away.' She felt too protective of her characters, the ones she'd brought into the world to palpitate and drive away the crowds. It wasn't their fault they'd been written.

Delphine would torture her with the imperfection of it all. She would read out some loose revelation, sip her coffee and look sympathetic. Then she would take five to compare the latest offering to 'The Artemis of Anchovy Beach', her favourite, the only one that wasn't a bush saga.

She couldn't bring herself to go in. What a pretty little terrace. What a piece of twee dell dum, all perky and wistful with wisteria. White and wunderbar with plenty of notices to the postperson. How could she go in. She felt just as gouged out as the building itself. A building that had vomited up its contents to make room for Rowena's Mayan antiques and exercise bike. Delph's domain owned a bullworker, and had signatures of famous people scrawled on its rustically plastered walls.

Hardacre growled when she considered her own prison on Malabar Road. She got angry at the thought of Val and Dan moving out of their Epping house because it was 'too big for them'. Poverty had driven them to 'Excalibur', where they'd been mugged so often they didn't need to go to the doctor for tranquillisers.

Hardacre had anticipated well the mood at Forget-Me-Not. Rowena and Delph had been placing their hopes on a move out of Lewisham, and into a more salubrious suburb. They had whispered McMahons Point into a deaf corporate ear. But the ailing profits of the company — thanks to bundles of assorted Hardacreage — pointed to economy measures. They would have to tighten their belts, cut back on cocktails, cancel freebies to Frankfurt, and publish fewer books in smaller type on ever faster disintegrating paper.

In fact the mood of the office was reptilean as Jane walked through the door. She hadn't seen them for five years, but their faces fell as if it were only yesterday. 'What have you got for us? Another sturdy Hardacre special? It looks thinner. It is thinner. What? You weren't serious about writing that serious novel? Now? At a time when we've been asked to concentrate on the coffee table?

'We thought you were joking when you said "something serious". But it's bound to be competent. We have great confidence in our authors. Not that we "do" much serious writing these days. We're tightening our belts, doing a lot of "how to" books for the gardener and home renovator. The romance list is flourishing.

'If it were only feminist, but I can tell at a glance it's not that. Never mind. I'm sure it's going to be marvellous. Everyone has at least one good book in them, and who's to say yours won't be serious. We'll have to send it out, of course, to as many readers as our budget will bear. You don't like that word, budget, do you Jane? Nobody does these days. I know five readers will be expensive and time wasting, but they are such a valuable cross-section of public taste. There is nothing like a committee decision to achieve excellence. As Rowena well knows, there are no egos in this office, no stars. Take away the capital and you could call us a co-operative. Women are much less power crazed than men. You should understand that Jane, locked away in your little attic, typing vigilantly like a medieval artisan. It must make you feel tremendously satisfied at the end of the day to know you're not chasing the dollar like everyone else. I envy my writers their innocence. I suppose I sound patronising? Rowena is always accusing me of being patronising. She keeps me honest. Would you like a coffee? We can't send you back to, where is it? Malabar, without a cup of coffee.

'Whatever you do, don't worry about the book. We'll get it back to you as soon as we can. Six months at the outside. I say that to cover us. More than likely we can give you an answer in three. What do I need to tell you these things for anyway? You know the ropes. You're not some pock-faced little idealist bringing in a first novel. I thank God for writers who know the ropes.'

Jane left feeling homicidal. If she hadn't known the ropes, she might've left feeling suicidal. She began to plan ways of doing her enemy in. D day. 'Pock-faced little idealists' would be grateful, so too the dusky Rowena waiting to step into the D day stilettos.

What end would be best? Feeding her to a book pulping truck? Draining out the brake fluid to make sure. Binding her into the binding of 'Prometheus Unbound'. Taking her out to meet Val and Dan's muggers at Liverpool. Giving her a Gatsby send off on an air bed. Wiring up her electric blanket to Wallerawang Sub Station? Hacking into her computer and commanding as many 'turkeys' as possible to reprint? The possibilities were endless.

'How will I ever be able to write full time?' Hardacre groaned. 'I know my country needs the blood of its authors, but even the regular army allows blood to be shed full time. Perhaps I should go back to the typing pool. That's if they'll employ someone greying, fraying, widening and moulting. "How could *she* qualify to grovel to fat cats in the second division?" they'd say. "How many sprays of duco will it take? She looks like a marlinless frump. An absolute cert for repetitive strain injury. Two months and compensation is in her eyes. Reckon she's had more typing hours behind her than she can take."'

Hardacre winced. Perhaps she should see a mortician before the interview. Even Italian shoes might not save her from unemployment. What was she going to do to keep herself out of debt?

There was always jackerooing in the Gulf Country, selling her body in some villainous country town where men smelt of cow and talked bull. Perhaps she could hide in a horse float heading up north — a photo finish to see who looked more amenable at the end of it all.

There, in the deep fried golden country, she might buy a fishing line to fish off the Great Barrier, enclosing the odd blue ringer in a padded post bag for Delph. She could give herself over to the simple pleasures of beachcombing, wending her way from one Japanese resort to the next, picking up bits of dead reef and giving them the kiss of life.

The kiss of life was what she needed, now dead and defeated on the 399 bus home. How would drivers cope with someone dying on the bus? Would they wait until the end of their shift before taking the corpse back to the depot?

Fortunately for her driver there were atavistic spasms left in her demoralised frame. Hardacre experienced the immense fatigue that went with rejection, the boredom of battle in a world without prizes.

Caught up in the tumbleweed of her own despair, Hardacre failed to notice a marlin gazing in her direction. The gorgeous creature was wearing an

Italian jumper and designer jeans. He exhibited concentrated interest. No doubt there was something nubile behind her, some piece of porn from a private girls school. Hardacre looked cautiously into the reflection in front to see who was sitting behing her. Gadzooks, there was an empty row. The marlin began to circle. Quelle chance. You like fraying, greying, dracos. Correction. You adore Hardacre — successful novelist, wit and raconteur. You've read one of my books? Recognise my face from that outrageously flattering jacket photo? Oh, er, you like 'The Artemis of Anchovy Beach'? Forgiven. Yes all is forgiven. What a spunk. I could lay down my life for you. Am I free? Always. Is this lack of oxygen I feel altitude sickness? Not the Regent. It's far too expensive! What kind of job do you have that you can afford the Regent? Oh . . . you're in publishing.

So much for being rescued from misery. Hardacre wateched her rejected marlin swim out to sea. It was not in her nature to woo the camp commandant. Had that beautiful creature been in any other walk of life, all would've been well, but there were times when beggars had to be choosers.

JANE WAITED and waited to hear from Delphine. Her new and even more mindless job in a laundry gave her time to think. In the evenings she knitted up sweaters for Val, balaclavas for Dan. It got nippy out west. There had been a committee decision not to instal central heating, so trade in woollies was brisk.

'It's not as though I've been trouble in the past,' Jane consoled herself as she worked. 'They know Hardacre is reliable at least, has a capacity for infinite industry. I have stacked up credibility like stamps from the supermarket. I demand you accept the serious novelist. For we are a race of wretched white brutes inhabiting the land, and someone has to make our excuses, recite the prayers no one will listen to.

'Where will we be down the track, when the gold diggers go? Is it not your nightmare dearest Delph that there is a sitting army of Hardacres all tapping away at our roots? I know I'm not alone. So stand up and be counted Delphine of the corporate dream. You can save yourself now. I'm giving you your chance mean Delphine of the Cointreau and cream. Take my book, publish it. Believe the passionate ones, readers who burn for the books. I beg you sweet Delphine, come clean and see what I mean.'

How could she? Delph of the corporate coma would never be won over. After nine months with the manuscript she moved it across her desk and into an out tray. 'I was surprised,' she told her author, 'that we had two good readers' reports because, quite frankly, I didn't like your book at all. As you know Jane, I like a more naturalistic approach, something I can relate to. That scene for example, where the mentally retarded boy jumps into a billabong to rescue the crocodile from the tourist. It stretches credibility. You say he wasn't mentally retarded. Well that's how he comes across. What do you think Rowena? Remember that boy in the Hardacre manuscript. Not the one with the limp—his friend—whose father was an arsonist. Not larcenist. Arsonist. The other one was a larcenist, had the built-up shoes, or was it a plate in his head, I can't quite remember. I don't want to make the whole thing sound worse than it was. I loved your dialogue, especially the dialogue in the third last chapter. You really capture the violence underlying Australian society. I must admit I had to think twice about some of the things you said. You might consider modifying some of your language though, just a few too many indiscreet words. Remember most readers are over forty.'

'Thanks to you they're over forty,' Hardacre wanted to say. Her chest muscles were too busy contracting to allow her further speech. Although her heart had stopped, her mind continued to race in all directions. Like many writers before her, some with even more years behind them, she began to snatch at compromise. Should I make it a picture book? Maybe my characters ought to pop out? Would it function in 3D, or as a series of holograms? Perhaps it could be made into a talking book that didn't swear? What must I do to see hard labour materialise?

Reading her thoughts, Delph smiled compassionately. 'The book needs a lot of re-writing. A lemon can't become a three course meal. Nor can Parkes be made into Paris. It would be silly of us to try to make Hardacre into Hemingway. Transformations of this nature are impossible. I repeat. Such transformations are impossible.'

'What must I do then?' Hardacre had found her voice, lost her pride. 'Just point me in the appropriate direction.'

'Point, my dear. It would take hours of editorial time, just when we're tightening our belts.'

'But you're so slim already. Delph give us a break.'

'How can I? I'm not accountable to writers you know.'

'I know my work is imperfect,' pleaded Hardacre. 'How many sessions will I need? Can I come before nine, or will I disturb the cleaners? How can I not make a nuisance of myself?'

'All right,' Delph paused. She was disturbed by her own lack of the killer instinct. 'With editorial assistance, we might be able to do something.'

'Spring clean the semantics,' enthused Hardacre, 'shake out the semiotics. Do things.'

'It needs some doing to. I'll have a conference with Rowena, the poor little thing is rather down in the mouth these days, and we'll see what we can come up with. You must give yourself over body and soul to our recommendations.'

'Either that, or I knit balaclavas full time.'

'We'll advance you, once the changes have been made, that is, if we're both happy about the book. Can't give guarantees at this stage.'

Delphine looked so pretty when she said things, even awful things. She was like a fairy godmother doing a soap commercial. Yet there was the liberated woman beneath. She told her marlen how to make love to her, read 'Cleo' from cover to cover, kept her figure muscular and trim. A few days with Delph took other women back into the dark ages, wanting to wear veils, or disappear into the masonry to contemplate their own unworthiness. For Delph played a round of golf off scratch, mixed aphrodisiacal cocktails, could sort out a stockbroker without buying lunch, knew enough politicians to lobby for an arc of child-care centres around her place of residence, when the time came. For she had no doubt that it would. And she would produce that perfect baby who could play its own Brahms lullaby on its junior violin. Her infant would be brilliant at maths and science, not losing marks for humanity in language or history. A neat little nobody speaking in the masonic sign language of higher mathematics, this thing would preach the theories of science as if they weren't going to be superseded in one generation. Eventually her darling would forsake science for the free market where it would apply its business skills. Then Delph's future would be assured. For at present her income was below what she felt she deserved. It was her fault, she recognised, for allowing herself to progress in an industry so undercapitalised. Now, stuck at the top as it were, she found herself on the branch of a shrub and not a tree. Many of her friends earned more than she did, which was why she was forced to keep her salary a secret. She didn't like having to keep secrets, nor did she like books very much. The problem with the industry was its concentration on books and writers. Writers were troublesome hacks, and sometimes she felt more like a publican than a publisher, always cleaning up the mess. That Hardacre book for example, it was unspeakably bad. Her prose was mutton when it could have been lamb. Un peu de pudeur was wanting, a pique de piquance that spoke of the joy of spring, gave the reader that abandonment, that sense of escape modern novelists so begrudged their readers. Prose should bring pleasure to people caught up in their immensely profitable careers, themselves looking down the jaws of the abattoir every day.

Writers like Hardacre, thought Delph, were consummate bores with their bags of knitting and arguments about *meaning*. When Hardacre crossed the threshold, plants went droopy, secretaries died and somebody usually burnt the element out of the jug. She was like a visit from the tax inspector. Even when she'd written junk it had been more like home made muesli than tasty fast food. The problem was she looked so pathetic, like something dragged up from the props department of an amateur theatre company. Ten minutes with Hardacre was like ten minutes in the cell of a condemned man. Her favourite colours were mustard and olive. She'd embarrassed them all by getting drunk at her launches, only thanking Valerie and Reg for coming from wherever it was. Her mother had worn pink woollen socks to the 'Artemis' launch, and Jane had looked down and giggled. The deathly silence that followed went unnoticed by the author who proceeded to sign all the launch copies of her book as 'Eva Perron'. Delphine winced. Writers were so infantile. People had been genuinely upset by her behaviour. Half the expected number of launch copies were sold. Delphine rummaged in the drawer for some hand lotion. Her hands felt unusually rough. Perhaps she'd been rubbing them together too much lately. Just because she was expecting a visit from Hardacre was no reason to give up on herself. Hands were important to a woman.

When Hardacre arrived, Delph gave her a few minutes to compose herself at reception. Jane was wearing a poncho with orange and green stripes. Her hair, limp and spiked, resembled a cactus with a disease. The synthetic shoes she was wearing made a rude squeaking sound on the floorboards. She looked angry and intense like someone demanding custody of a child from the wrong chamber magistrate.

'Come in Jane,' reproached Delphine. 'You look lost.' Her Sophia Loren eyes narrowed as if to say 'No need to grovel, dear, you'll get your $3000 advance.'

'Come in Rowena, too. You're just the person we need.'

Hardacre sighed faintly. Together, Rowena and Delph were unbeatable. They worked like a pair of well trained sheep dogs, nipping at the heels of their authors, lunging at their throats, getting them onto their woolly backs. 'Take your eyes off my poncho,' Jane warned. Their businesslike contempt kept her pinned down and fixed in one position.

In tandem this pair had unique authority and grace. Whilst Delphine talked constantly about 'the bestseller', Rowena explained the fickle public to despairing authors. She painted a picture of treachery and betrayal bleaker than a promotions budget for a first novel. The market place was no place for books. Nobody liked books unless they were down in the mouth Jeremiahs living in inner city squats. People didn't have time to read. Life today was all about making enough money in ten years to see one through thirty years of retirement. Books, because of their arrogant time scale, were an admission of failure in the modern world. A symbol of collective impotence as they passed on the secrets of human weakness from one generation to the next. If they had any use at all it was to ward off evil spirits, lock up bad luck between covers. But what kind of selling point was that?

For these reasons, neither Delphine nor Rowena enjoyed reading. For them, exorcism had to be painless and swift. What sound was more plaintive than the beating of authorial wings against corporate plate glass. 'The poor creatures can't stop once they start. We shoo them away, but its useless, they are programmed to become nuisances.'

Although Delphine and Rowena were bored by reading, editing was another matter. Editing, for them, was all about the exercise of personal authority, deflating writers all puffed up with their delusions like proud parents at a parent-teacher night. Most books needed re-writing, at least they were accepted for publication on that basis. A healthy distrust of all forms of creativity was essential to the Forget-Me-Not editor. And—from the financial point of view—the smaller the imagined stakes, the more rigorous could be the bookkeeping. Delph would spare no effort to save costs on Hardacre, whilst a businessman writing his profitless and altruistic memoirs could run up all the overheads he liked. There was, after all, an army of Hardacres working to subsidise his efforts.

'Now Jane,' Delphine began the autopsy. 'I don't want to deliver my usual sermon. The one I give to newchums in the writing game. But speak I must. Speak about that perfect book that every serious writer is committed to. I know you have said in the past that I like everything foreign, but you're mistaken there. I really favour the vignette, some metaphorical piece of joyous turf from anywhere. Of course aimless foppery from the English upper classes is amusing. And our Australian short stories are excellent, they're so short. Literature should not overtax. Governments do that for us. The job of a serious novelist is to advertise the truth, persuade us indirectly. Life may beat us about the ears with a blunt instrument, but literature should deaden the pain, put gloves on the strangler, if you'll excuse my extemporisation. Jane, I am advising you to flow with the current. Cast your net out into the river of life, bring in your images without tangling the net. Be effortless and unforced. Don't go looking for sharks in the estuary. Do you see my point? Might I also add that genre is a girl's best friend. Sci-Fi thrillers, detective stories, rural sagas. I always think of genre as shoulder padding. Quite invaluable to she who wants to cut a dash.

'What I am leading up to my dear is your confusion.

The book is neither comedy nor tragedy. It metamorphises from one into the other. Let us call it passionate farce, rather than farcical passion. Passion is often a problem in the novel, rather like body odour. People resent infringements on their privacy, a stranger standing too close and peering over their shoulder while they read. A distance is always desirable. Jane you must learn to keep your distance. I don't mean it literally, of course.

'Now that leads me into the next problem. Your vulgarity. I admit that vulgarity is the hallmark of great Australian literature. But it is ironic, in control. To give you one example: it might be acceptable to fart around a campfire, but a similar indiscretion amid the glassware at Prouds is unforgivable. There is a literary tradition surrounding the campfire, but farting in Prouds is sheer vulgarity.

'Jane. I don't like your characters. I'm not referring to Prouds again. They are too vulnerable, morbid. People just aren't like that. They don't agonise over loveless lives. They don't have lice phobias and cry themselves to sleep at nights. Most people are too busy to think, that's the way they like it. They put things on the tab, running total or whatever. They get tinea and threadworms. They spread their anger, like good fertiliser, across their lives. Your central character, I don't like to pry, but is she based on your own experience? Really? Well I do think she's overdone.

There aren't many women I know who have no sex appeal whatsoever. Most have a twinkle in the eye, if you know what I mean. But Jane, you provide no twinkles. Your central character is full of fear. She is not likable. How can you expect us to sell the book in America? Your character is the personification of poverty without hope. Hope is the sun over there, and some worship it like a false god in the anticipation their luck will change. If you can imagine a Christian casino, Jane. Hope is the currency, therein lies its power. You are depriving people of hope, which is most unChristian of you. The point you make about hope and humility being at odds is fallacious.

'And as life is rarely bizarre, fiction should not concentrate on the surreal either. Life isn't bizarre, is it Rowena? If it were, then things might be a bit more interesting around here. Life is all about the small tragedies. Unemployment, families, corporate take-overs, mid-life crises.

'Your style. Jane I hesitate to quibble. Your style is all wrong. Puddings are out of fashion my dear. A Hardacre page is heavy with raisins and suet. Your images fall upon each other like schoolboys in a ruck — gratuitously, dangerously. I showed it to Martin and he agreed. Martin's read "Hansard" from cover to cover. Who says men don't read? Anyway to return to the book. What exactly are you trying to say? Rowena pass me the hand lotion. My hands still feel rough. I don't know what's wrong with them at the moment. They look so blue and cold. Look at them Weenie, don't they look cold. It can't be circulatory. I'm too young for circulatory problems. Back to the book. I think your central character is too close to you, Jane. I'm not saying *like* you, merely close to you. There's the rub, all I like and they're still blue. I agree that in the end, life cannot give us what we want. There are times too when I could give up. Sometimes I wake up in the mornings and ask myself "What's it all about?" But then I look into the mirror to remind myself of my responsibilities to myself. I say: "I owe this person more than indifference and defeatism. This is me, Delphine, mine. I must nurture her with all her faults as God's gift." You, Hardacre, have the same responsibility. With your talent to create life, you smash the mirror, bite the hand that feeds you. If you're going to take writing seriously then don't take out your infantile revenge on the human condition. You're only cutting off your nose to spite your. . . . Look at my hands. They're quite a dark shade now, a definite violet.

'What I liked about "Artemis" was its positive outlook on life. It was different from your bush sagas. You take the reader with you, down to Anchovy Beach with its sights and sounds. I can still hear the waves roaring. See the children in their old-fashioned sunsuits. Smell the salt and suntan oil. Touch the sunburnt flesh of boys and girls. Feel the anguish of a mother deciding between her children and her career as an actress. So real. And that gigolo with a bullworker the same brand as mine. A masterpiece. I begged Martin to read it. Anyway let's not dwell on past glories. We must live in the here and now. . . .'

By the time Hardacre had left Delph's office, she felt like an insect without a sting. Delph had triumphed. But Jane, in spite of the diatribe, would not give in to the tactics of the Delphic mentor, menteuse. A woman like Delph could be worn down by a Hardacre emery board—a writer who insisted on artistic integrity, who brought body odour into the office until they thought warm days would never cease. In the end, it would be she, Hardacre, who would prove the most determined, sustained by the knowledge that any ill will she bore the human condition could be exorcised in Delph's office, defending the right to exercise ill will against the human condition.

The real problem was Val and Dan. Val was growing thin and Dan fat, since their move out west. They lived on porridge and mince. They were ashamed of themselves and told how the other old folks in the village thought them rather rag-picky with their marlinless daughter, pension cheques cashed two seconds after delivery at great speed down to the post office.

Of course Dan was making a little money now

washing cars. Val took in ironing. But these things only paid for life's little extravagances — take-away Chinese, support panty hose for Val on her feet all day, the tom cat that called in for a feed. Such a soft touch those two, victims of the disease of old age — sentimentality. As they lost brain cells they gained friends.

WHEN HARDACRE at last worked up the courage to re-read her manuscript, she was horrified. Delph had been right, for all the wrong reasons. It was dreadful, truly dreadful. The central character disappeared under an avalanche of imagery. Her suicide at the end reassured the reader she would never appear in print again. What was the bloody thing all about? There was no point of view. What had she, Hardacre, to say about a human condition that had so callously shunned her, frozen her out as she tried to understand.

She'd attempted to cut a diamond with an axe. Humbler mortals might have been content to let the diamond sparkle in the sun. (She felt as humble as a mortal could get, but perhaps it wasn't humble to think like that.)

The book needed a complete overhaul. It was too

picaresque, a series of adventures that became anti-climaxes, and thus devalued experience, particularly the life of her character. Just because life was a series of anti-climaxes did not mean she had to write that way, with each image one upping the next in order to convince the public that reading was better than watching television. Let them have the box. She would occupy her Hardacreage, building a fence around the human condition with one eye on the horizon.

Positive thinking was what she needed. She was sick of talking herself down. Nothing had value until it was talked up on the free market. Whilst selling herself she had to look relaxed, altruistic and generous. If she loved books enough she could court her readers as the eternal lover—always young, ever enthusiastic and ready to sacrifice all but passion and a state of mind.

Hardacre decided to buy an expensive suit and briefcase. She would re-write her bad novel and get the better of Delph in the conference room. She might have a flirt with the occasional marlin, enjoy more time with Val and Dan, go to the hairdresser, send a generous contribution to Amnesty International, buy cocktails at expensive hotels, catch taxis, fill the bath to maximum capacity, live on credit, buy new underwear, paint the flat, indulge in a weekly massage. Flog the old bank account for the dead horse it was.

For she had a plan. Years of isolation and self discipline had forged new resolve. Forged was the appropriate word. She had a surprise in store for Delphine the literature queen. At their next editorial conference she would listen to every word, take notes like a round shouldered biographer, and compliment Delph on her mistressy of the English language. Hardacre would practise making her eyes go magnetic and intense, like people did on television. She would research obscure cocktails until she found one in illuminated manuscript form. Then she would tell Delph that it was all the rage, and make embarassed excuses on her publisher's behalf.

Whilst she 'wrote notes', she could be planning out her new book. For Hardacre had had a wonderful idea. Instead of deceiving herself, she would deceive her publisher. She would write two books. One bad one for Forget-Me-Not, and a little gem which she could take to another publisher. The books would have the same title, and thus the over-promoted turkey would subsidise the under-promoted gem. It seemed to Hardacre that subversion was the only logical course.

First, there was work to be done. Her mental and moral guttering needed clearing. Three days' fast. Sleep. A new blade for the razor. Knitting aborted. Clean windows. Meditation. Erotic literature — something translated from Latin in fragrant fragments.

From as early as next week, she would be unrecognisable. Transformation was in the air like an excess of pollen. She could feel her spine straightening, hair

curling, skin clearing, mind sharpening. Change made the air heavy, full of dignified humidity.

Her flat took on the sobering aspect of a council chambers. She had work to do, pleasure to engage in. She would have to ferret out the hard working parts in her personality and accept the responsibilities that went with abandonment.

When she put on her suit of finest cashmere, and wore her dearest hose, no one would recognise her. That was unless she chose to reveal herself—La Phantome—Ghostess who walks, she who never dies. . . .

For until now she'd laboured long in the vineyard. She'd punished herself like a true Victorian—working words and images like undersized infants in a mill. Her last book had taken her youth—6 am–7 pm (the Victorians would have approved of that baker's dozen, they who'd worked their characters until they dropped dead in harness on page 600). It was a cruel age which had left a cruel legacy—the sentimentality of the 'likable' character, and books that went on too long.

Nowadays, felt Hardacre, it was not a question of working an image, merely occupying it, giving it something to do until the time came. It was an age of effortlessness, weightlessness. Images had to appear unforced, naked, natural. Nobody wanted to sit down to unhook their way through a corset to the truth beneath. Words had to dance and sing about ideas, for ideas dance like light, a distant shimmering on a desert road.

Hardacre knew she would have to abandon that Victorian professionalism which she'd so admired and which had mummified her own muse. From now on, her prose would have to proceed like a swaggie. Beg from door to door. For her income did not justify the label 'professional'. Being 'professional' was a lie—it stifled the author in the way that the title 'governess' suffocated intelligent women a century before.

'WHAT DO YOU mean you agree?' Delph fell back vanquished on her Danish love seat with the amorous wheels. 'My God you've changed. Where's your poncho? You know Jane, I liked you as you were. There was something so poignant about a writer who gave herself over so wholly to her work. Now you seem, dare I say it, a little streamlined. I'd grown fond of those little blue moustaches of yours, those carbonated fingers.

'Sometimes you'd leave my office and a wonderful peace would descend, like the peace that follows in the wake of a mystic. I know mystics have a place in other societies which is possibly more secure than yours. I appreciate your need to conform. You do look different I must say. But spare a thought for the plain Jane of "Artemis" fame. Don't become callous my dear. It's made me quite lyrical this loss. She may have been frumpy (I can be frank now you look so different), but she was so real, vulnerable, absent-minded, generous, all the things Rowena and I treasure in a writer. Of course you can't have changed deep down. And deep down you always were a go-getter, rather like me, which was why we had to argue from time to time. The more I think about it, the more I like the new Jane. Don't you Weenie? She's the real Jane. Val and Dan won't know you. Still visiting Sundays? I love your suit. They were all the rage in New York last fall. I adore cashmere. It has such an old fashioned quality to it — like a well-embroidered tray cloth, a handkerchief from Bruges.

'I can't say I was ready for you to accept all my recommendations. I'm not an artist after all. If I could teach writers how to do their jobs I'd be a wealthy woman. But in the end it's up to them to come to their senses. It's their risk, and yours, Jane.

'It will mean re-writing everything but the third last chapter. I won't say "re-draft", that would be dishonest. The book needs a complete overhaul. Are you ready for it? We'll take it chapter by chapter? Have I got the time? you ask. Most managing directors are still sub-editing manuscripts. Up to their elbows in grease they will always remain.

'In short, Jane, I have the time. I think you will approve of the new story line, unless you think it resembles "Anchovy" too much. There are some "Anchovian" elements of course, but the book will have a life of its own. I thought we'd centre it on the character of the gigolo who comes into money of his own. I like that idea. It has that essential Cinderella ingredient. He will then take awful and systematic revenge on a stream of middle-aged lovers.

'I suggest we do one chapter a month. It's better to do things in stages—you impetuous artists throw caution to the wind—but investors break wind in such a situation. Life is all about cash flow for them, spreading their costs. I still have to work on behalf of my bosses, wherever they might be. What do artists know about economics? Your offer to do a part-time business course does not impress. You ask what might economists know about books? It is a question of individuals. And I do not agree that more artists understand economics than economists understand art.

'Writers like to think of themselves as special. Everyone can write. Some choose to write, others don't. But not everyone can understand the vicissitudes of the market place. We are not born with that ability. So I suggest we proceed in stages. Chapter by chapter. You remark on my hands. I have to wear gloves because

I've developed a skin condition. There's no cause for alarm. According to my doctor I have some kind of hormonal imbalance which in due course can be rectified. If you must know, Jane, I have a rather embarassing problem which I am at present attempting to conceal. If it were anyone else I'd be too ashamed to tell them. As it's you, I suppose I can be frank. Recently I've noticed my body changing. My skin has become bluish and an excess of body hair has flourished on my back and hands. My nails have grown into points, and it's difficult to spread my fingers. I can still hold a coffee cup, do the things I have to do. Thank God it's only a temporary problem, and when I see you next I'll be sure to report significant improvement. Has Rowena seen my hands, you ask? No. The hair is extremely coarse. It's come as quite a shock. I'm not used to being coarse, hideous. It's un-me.

'It's come as quite a shock. And the "thousand hairs that flesh is heir to" is a joke in bad taste, Jane. I see you haven't lost that delightful vulgarity of yours. And the hair is apparent. Yes very good. You can go on punning at my expense for hours. Writers never grow up. It's their fatal charm. I went to bed with a writer once. So unfit, but so full of charm, I forgave him for his performance. They are charming, disappointing creatures, always inventing excuses for themselves. Anyway I'm condemned to wearing gloves, my dear Jane, leaving proof without print. There. That's my little contribution to the punning game. I'll see you next month, when we can discuss your revised first chapter.

HARDACRE WORKED on her two books, the one for Delph that would fail, and the other one. It would never be difficult to write a failure, and with Delph's facility for miscalculation, it was assured. For Delph supervised one failure after another. Promotion costs negated even her successful pieces of ephemera. Her bestsellers, she boasted, made their one million, she never mentioned the $950,000 in costs. Relatively speaking, quality writers made more money. However they looked shabby on the revenue side of the budget, rather like petty cash.

Hardacre smiled. Her failure would be a farewell present to Rowena and Delphine. First she would extract a handsome advance because of their misplaced confidence. Then she would serve up the dross they wanted, skipping off into the night with something of great beauty and worth under her arm.

She would write no saga. For in truth, each

generation in Australia disowned the other. Still convicts they sought to form no bonds with those who occupied the cell before. Dear Val and Dan were her friends, and loved for that reason. They boasted no past and claimed no future.

Hardacre wanted to try her new, southern, voice. Deaf and dumb for years, her vocal chords would sound inhuman, animalistic in the beginning. People might laugh at her, find her passionate grunting pathetic. But she was tough, and new, and the world was running out of time.

The advance paid by Forget-Me-Not would take her, Val and Dan on a holiday. Destination: the Blue Lake at Mount Gambier, across to the Flinders Ranges and onto the sublime north west. She would buy a caravan. Perhaps one day they would do all of Highway 1. She imagined them cavorting somewhere inland. Three in the nuddy near a waddy close to paddy melons. Salt drifting across them like chadors and wild cotton. Spinifex to tickle, acacia to torture, tumbleweed to roll them across and under the horizon. The caravan would tow them like a bull ant pulling its load, to its proud clay castle, its stalagmite pushing up to the sky to jemmy rain out from the blue vault and onto the dry earth below where cracks are canyons and ants learn to wind their way like patient pilgrims towards the sky.

Words spilled out like frogs, as instantaneous as the

rain. Hardacre looked around herself. If self respect had come with difficulty, words were showing no such reluctance. Like a child she had too much to say. And like a child she was all breath and conjunctions. She crossed out 'ands' and all manner of irrelevancy. At the end of Chapter 12 (her last, according to the floor plan she was writing), she would look for her marlin. Like a child she had a tendency to repeat herself. She would search him out between drafts. Then, asserted Hardacre, she would attempt a flirtation. She would sink into the sensuous interlude like a geisha, enjoying her free time over the New Year. This would mean deliberate self abandonment. Difficult for someone shy to the point of retardation. She was no Delphine with well oiled sphincter — tried and true routines for fulfilling men's dreams. Her bedroom patter would resemble more the clawing of a possum come inadvertently down a chimney to piss itself and panic. Stop, recall the new Jane. The new Jane would be charmingly awkward, proud of her inexperience, curious. The new Jane would take off her clothes cautiously and systematically without tangling, pretending nothing mattered when underwear was inside out. The new Jane would tease her lover, compliment him, and make the compliments convincing by complaining about the horror of the human condition.

From now on the new Jane would believe in the power of the word, and the power of the word to change. For in each character lay the secrets of humanity — a little tin box of treasures rattling in time to Bach. Painted, written, sung, the word would remain as mysterious as communication, the unquenchable loneliness that like a spring refreshes all but the spring itself.

HARDACRE WORKED demonically throughout the month. She exploited divisions in her personality, played them off one against the other to produce the Delphic and divine manuscripts. She had followed Delph's instructions to the letter. The plot outline and first chapter were ready. The plot outline was detailed — a real starling's nest of cliches. The gigolo, doubly potent since his inheritance, plots revenge on a wealthy widow. He takes her to bed, but fails to complete delivery. She screams abuse, he calls her a rotting bag of manure, packs up the tools of his trade, and leaves. He writes a farewell note informing the old dear that she's been poisoned, has ten minutes to make it to intensive care, and will not have time to get dressed. The widow puts on her diamonds, emerald tiara, and rings for an ambulance to come immediately. She's too sick to put on her clothes. The ambulance arrives five minutes late. The widow and her diamonds are covered in vomit at the foot of a sweeping Georgian staircase. Uggh. What vile happenings. Such ugliness would never sell. For Delph, the public mind was as low as a sawn off coffee table. Each chapter would see something more subtracted, an inch or so, sawn off and sanded until by the end of the book there were no legs, only a lid, a coffin lid resting on the ground with outrageous purposelessness.

Her real book would show faith in transformation. Show people trying to be better against their better judgment. It would talk of love in a dry continent, how it came not out of sweet lubricity, but fearful complicity with the world.

She would show the convicts in their spiritual hold emerging. Bullied into love in their new country. Thunder and lightning their real overlords, the sexes unable to talk, and many a false showing in a world without rain.

It struck Hardacre that by at last giving Delph the thing she wanted, she was forgiving her in some way. Obedience was forgiveness, possible only for the person with something up her sleeve—God, a manuscript, a lover. All three. Obedience was an expression of the power of forgiveness, having very little to do with humility.

JANE'S NEXT meeting with Delph was unremarkable, but for the bone she found on her seat. It was not a large bone, but something splintered and well-picked. Delph jumped up and growled at Jane as she tried to remove it, but seeing that she looked ridiculous, contented herself with sinking back into her chair. She still wore her gloves, gloves that had two fingers missing and were filled with material of some kind. A rare skin disease indeed, thought Hardacre. The woman's got leprosy and refuses to accept treatment.

It would not suit Delph to contract a gross and antiquated disease. No doubt she would deny everything. Poor Delph. Her nose was looking rather squashed. And as for her face, it seemed to be growing forward.

The heaviness of Delph's makeup disguised skin which was blue, and a muzzle which was becoming hirsute. Not quite 'muzzle', but her features were moving inexorably towards the canine.

'Delph, what's happened to you?' whispered Hardacre. 'This skin disease of yours appears most troublesome. Are you sure it's being treated in the right way? You talk inaudibly. And I take it you grunt approvingly at my work. What does Rowena advise? She seems rather pleased. And your marlen? Have they noticed any changes? You tell me not to concern myself, but Delph, things look serious. Your arms are shorter. I swear they're a good four inches less than they were.

You say as soon as you shave your legs the hair springs back immediately. That's not right, nor will it do.

'I see you've given me a new outline for the next eleven chapters. I suspect it's because you're about to go into hospital. Don't worry I'll discard what I've written and start again. O Delph, dear Delph. Why must we all learn the hard way. I am not such a vengeful creature that I want you to suffer. A hysterectomy would have done.

'But this? What does Weenie say about it? I promise to follow those chapter outlines religiously. You say don't come back until the first draft is finished. I must respect your need for privacy. You think it's a temporary ailment, that eight fingers will see you through. I hope you're right.

'You can't stand up? Is it because your legs are so much shorter? That Italian suit, always so impeccable, appears to be chewed. I can promise you it still looks wonderful. Don't worry, please. But the jacket has unravelled, and the skirt has puckered like a dry mandarin. Can I fix some of these threads hanging down for you? I'm sorry. If you want me to keep my distance I will. There's no need to show your teeth. Speaking of which your molars have benefited from the curtailment of other parts. They are white and quite magnificent. It is obviously not a calcium deficiency which plagues you.

'Weenie, I'm glad you've come in. I need some

moral support. Delphine is seriously ill, don't you agree? Perhaps it's a mental condition, wreaking physical havoc. Lycanthropy. Take off the 'lyc', and leave the canthropy. You have a syndrome where the sufferer believes herself a dog.

'Perhaps she has gone to a movie friend to aid her psychosis, asked the makeup department to turn her into a blue heeler. The science of disguise is advanced nowadays. I know it's not a practical joke, because Delph is the kind to take things seriously.

'What are we going to do? I really don't think you should speak to her like that, snapping your fingers and ordering her to sit up. You are exploiting her sickness. The poor creature is sniffling. Look at her. Or is it sniffing? My God she has begun to unbutton her blouse. Stop it Delph. I say stop it. At least, you say, your stomach is hairless, and Rowena stroking it like that.

'Whether you like it or not, I'm not going to button you back up, and there's no point licking me indecently down there. Weenie tells me you've pissed on your cocktail shaker. Let me finish. It's not polite to urinate in public. Your tongue is so long. Put it back. You're a disgrace to the name "publisher". When I think how squeamish you used to be; now you seem content to live amongst puddles as if they were the prettiest of lilypads.

'Shame on you. Rowena you're not helping, stroking

her, aiding and abetting the transformation with lust in your eyes. She is making you, too, into a wild creature. I feel we owe her something more than curiosity. Take your hands off, tweaking the poor dark nipples, playing with her ears all soft and droopy like end of season ferns. Weenie, you're dancing on her grave.

'A nail protrudes from the poor creature's gloves. I think we can take them off now. What *are* we going to do? Is there any hope for she who has violated the word? Or is the mistake too literal?

'Time's getting on, anyway. I've got to get back to my book. Delph, let me apologise to you. I feel disposed to laugh. You dangle between two worlds — a typographical error on galley proofs — a widow. Delph, unless you acknowledge your condition, there will be no remission. You say you're happy, that dog can be spelled backwards. I wish you well.

'Don't see me to the door. Save your strength. I beg to be excused from this obsequy on all fours. Stand up Delph. Have your forgotten how? You tell me your marlen still enjoy you. Shame on them. I say, shame. Weenie, she's spilled her Manhattan all over herself. Please, wipe her snout — nose, I'm sorry. I really am sorry. A hysterectomy would have done. But you know her eyes are soft. Look, Weenie — soft and cunning. I don't dislike the way they look. You say she's still mean. It's hard to believe. I see great humanity. Take her for walks, won't you? By the look of her files, so neatly stacked, Delph is still very much in control.

'We all change. Do you think I could borrow her shoes? She seems to be using those football socks now. Weenie your feet are so tiny. They fit me like a glove, speaking of which, shouldn't we take off the gloves now, the seams have come apart.

'Quite frankly, friends, I thought over a certain age life would hold no surprises. But here I am witnessing the strangest events. It gives me renewed faith in the world. Who would have guessed that Delph could show me the miraculous, those wonders she is still denying in herself? The woman is a treasure. If she becomes too much for you Weenie, I'll take her home. Worm her Weenie. Keep her office clean. She doesn't need those reading glasses anymore. I suggest you take the phone calls from now on. Her critical faculties seem as sharp as ever, and I see she still enjoys a good romance.

'Can't stay much longer (have to check that the foundations of my masterpiece have set). Take her to the vet regularly, won't you? Catch you down the track Ween. By the way, I wouldn't keep her locked up too much, the odd day trip, business lunch, would do her the world of good.'

HARDACRE LEFT Forget-Me-Not in a state of sublime detachment. Nothing seemed to matter anymore, except her book. She had been planning it for quite a while. Every twist and turn of the narrative road was known to her, but no doubt the route would change.

She would have to keep Delph a secret, as nobody would believe her anyway. Perhaps one day it would become part of white woman's dreaming: How the Delph was lost for Words.

Leastways, no one would believe her. For she was a Hardacre. Hardacres who lived on Malabar Road lead boring lives, boring, marlenless lives. At the moment, it didn't matter. She had two books to write — the Delphic novel to be lain at the feet of the goddess transformed, and 'Black Guitar'.

The desire for continuity was something she couldn't explain. It went beyond self preservation, was a need that separated humankind from the beast. A desire not merely to communicate, but to record and hand down in some form. Hardacre wondered at this magic seed planted in the species, how it could grow and flourish, how it could mutate and corrupt.

Poor Delph. Hardacre imagined a magician-come-writer furled in black crepe. His assistant, Delphine, all legs and leotard has become a spy for an international corporation of accountants and magicians. In order to prove life's magic, the assistant has had to be sacrificed. Whoosh . . . Woof. Delph's fishnets hang loose like it's Boxing Day at an orphanage. The audience applauds. Delph pisses on the imperial purple drapes, and fades into comic relief. Her corporate bosses (one of whom is in the audience) are not displeased. Now she is an even more faithful employee, and one who can be so readily put down.

Hardacre tried to imagine the decisions Delph would have to make. Would she be happy to chase cats? Or would it be a bit of a bore—like Thursday night shopping. Would her sex life get even better? Or would she become a canine recluse?

The only other transformations of note Hardacre had witnessed were local. There was the Daceyville postman who, off duty, dabbled in the occult. And there was the man in her block who, after his wife died, covered his body in multicoloured tattoos of platypii.

Her real book had to deal with change. The disguises some people used as dress rehearsals for change. Delph had been the least canine of creatures. More fastidious than a Siamese, she'd loathed all shagginess and signs of panting loyalty. Most people adopted disguises out of sheer necessity, but in Delph's case there had been elements of perverse denial there. Like a child holding back its Freudian play poo, Delph had held back on words. She'd denied them, and their purveyors, warmth and love. She'd stored up magic inside her like a kadaitcha, only concerned with obscuring his own tracks. She'd stored up magic like a miser, and abracadabra it had turned her inside out.

What would the Forget-Me-Not authors be told? Delph has left for England suddenly, to take a promotion? They would then ask Weenie to send their congratulations on, hoping that Weenie would prove kinder than her contracts, kinder than the oracle itself.

Most authors, Hardacre suspected, would dance on Delph's demise as if they felt warm days would never cease. 'Is this the new dispensation?' they might ask. 'The second coming down under where we writers can nudge the nipple of human kindness and find a flow. For we the underpaid are the peacemaker souvenir sellers in a country of ghosts. We buy and sell time's leftovers, subsidised by the government if the climate is right. O successor, be kind to the intransigent oracle herself. New in mate, cast off your crimsoned robes and lay them folded at the feet of justice. If you find a juvenile manuscript, allow some time for it to grow. And most of all we beseech you, do not delay, by sending poor Habeas Corpus away. He is a most well meaning gent, and does not like manuscripts returned after months, unread.

'For we say to the new Delph, whoever she might be: "You are a printer's broker, an administrator with some civil responsibility. Your lack of courtesy and inhuman delays will not be tolerated. One day we will be tempted to take our books straight to the humble printer. Tempted by the ease of the subcontract, we say no to our texts being laundered, laundered by crims. So take off your crimsoned robes you toads and make amends.'"

Is that what Delph's authors would say? And since when are book corporations arbiters of public taste? Hardacre wanted to ask on her own account. They are bookies playing the futures, not bookmen looking to the future. One thing she felt was for sure: the new Delph would need a degree of humanity and literacy if she didn't want her molars to grow.

Hardacre's enthusiasm for 'Black Guitar' expressed itself in a dedication to Val and Dan, the first book she'd dedicated to anybody. Weenie's novel, the bad one, could be locked away like Dorian's portrait—the uglier and more sordid it became, the more beautiful the other would seem.

She wanted to write the story of a black country and western singer who, in Gondwanaland his country of ghosts, plays the music of the white trash who live across the sea.

He bootlegs from town to town. It is still prohibition in most bars for him, in essence, if not fact. He drinks freely, yet guiltily, singing the white music from over the sea. It is only through this music of hardship and foreign feeling that he can find common ground. A nomad in a Texan hat, he receives the ambiguous pawings of others at the bar. For around these new waterholes there's as much disputation as ever, and he has to play the gracious newcomer singing for his supper.

He likes to move about, for the wisdom of ancestral animals teaches charity. Keep moving and you'll keep forgiving. He follows dreaming tracks like dance steps to the horizon, trailing a non-koori behind him like his horse. He takes her to see his only living relatives, Valerie and Dan under different aliases, living on a settlement and scolding the young ones for their misdemeanours.

Hardacre, what part of you is in this young man? Do you seek transformation for yourself, or everyone else? Make yourself a coffee, for fancy's a deceiving self. Make it strong and black, for that is where the strength lies. You must draw from it with gratitude and humility. It is yours to acknowledge.

So HARDACRE worked with all her strength for two years. During this time Val received the Order of Australia for her contribution to knitting, and Dan suffered from prostate. Jane's neighbours had packed up and left for the Central Coast, to continue their urban warfare in a milder climate.

Rowena took all the phone calls now, reassuring Jane that she was taking good care of Delph. 'Your manuscript must be ready,' she said to Jane. 'I know we've kept you waiting most cruelly in the past. But this manuscript was to be Delph's pride and joy.'

So Hardacre posted the commissioned dross to Weenie, and went back to work on the one for the other publisher.

'I'm so grateful, Jane,' said Rowena, 'for all the trust you've shown in us over the years. We've read the book, although you only posted it last week. We do so love it, love everything but the title. I don't think "Black Guitar" is appropriate for a story of love and revenge. It's too downbeat. However as you are so insistent about it, I think we can let it through. Your book is a triumph. I love the way the gigolo terrorises the bridge club, and that scene where he drives his Triumph through the window of a surgical aids shop, and ends up trussed up. It's a masterpiece. You know I am so heartily sick of books which fail to entertain.

'Ploughing through a modern novel is like cutting one's way through a religious tract. All unctuousness and typographical errors. I sometimes wish I could remind writers of their duties to the reader. They blame the publisher for their lack of success, when all along it is their own dreary prose.

'There isn't one serious writer in our list who can make me laugh. They are all too busy peddling vignettes—the tram systems in St Kilda, the coffee shops in Darlinghurst. Realism is vulgarity when not describing Hampstead or Maida Vale. Those places have an exoticism which refines experience, people are lifted by wit and erudition. In Australia we aren't solid. Not enough history behind us, only the sandbags you see propping up sets in cheap soap operas.

'"Black Guitar" is delightfully surrealistic. Some might say that it is escapism, but not I. Surrealism is perfect for those who have no reality, no cultural identity. It is amusing, it makes no demands. And yours, Jane, has the advantage of being a conte morale. What a little gem. You have such a light touch. I mean it. We're going to promote Delph's, your, book to the hilt. Publisher's budgets are always limited, but we thought some newspaper advertising. You want just the title displayed? I don't see why not. It'll save on design costs. We've got to co-operate, haven't we Jane? We share a little secret. Only you and I know about our canine friend, chained to her desk. I thought you might like to take her home now the transformation is complete. She makes such a pretty blue heeler, don't you think? A pretty smoky blue. She's still kept those lovely facial bones of hers. Built like a true athlete. I don't think she'd go home with anyone but you.'

So HARDACRE and her heeler left for Malabar Road. The dog, a true baskerville, strained at the leash. Her demonic eyes flashed at all who passed by. Occasionally she'd turn round and try to nip Jane, her head bowing like a sleek seal. It was a long walk back to the eastern suburbs, but Delph did not notice, she had two extra legs. There was still a fastidiousness about her, spring-loaded and neat. She couldn't pass another dog without lunging at its throat. Then, after a few seconds, she'd abandon her victim with distaste, as though she'd copped a dud oyster at an exclusive restaurant.

When she pissed she squatted daintily, watching where the stream went so she need not dabble her paws. Some people who passed Jane and her dog in the street couldn't help exclaiming: 'What a magnificent specimen. Just listen to that Lauren Bacall bark.' Delph would then turn shy and feminine producing a muted version, hollow-throated and womanly, of that distinctive heeler sound.

'Are you happy now, Delph?' Hardacre asked. But the creature shook its head stubbornly, refusing to indicate one way or the other. Delph was already learning to use the mystique of her species. Her eyes displayed the uncanny subterfuge of a mid-summer snake. Her muscular body was as sinewy as a Moreton Bay. The footpath was her veldt, she used every inch of it—as if it were a newly declared game park, and she felt fettered by its boundaries.

'Stop straining Delph. We've got five miles to go.' But Delph was in no mood to listen. Quite frankly, the thought of living on Malabar Road did not appeal. In Hardacre's shabby unit she would feel like a criminal in hiding. If she were discovered the body corporate would insist she be put down.

As far as Delph was concerned, she was the sort of dog one 'showed'. The kind paraded by a docile owner, awarded points, fondled by judges, watched enviously by inferiors. Hardacre was a liability of maddening proportions. As an owner, she had all the charisma of children's book week. No doubt she'd be the kind of person who'd expect her to fetch a ball. The idea appalled. She would have to dispose of all balls at the first opportunity. Fetching, rolling over, begging, pleading for walks, gulping down dinner were crossed off the agenda. She was no do-good, retrieving, class-pet-collie of a lissome thing. She detested Hardacre and her compassionate jerking on the leash.

If she hadn't needed an owner, she would have torn out Hardacre's throat. But she knew all too well that dogs, even of her calibre, were not in demand when stalking the streets. The best thing she could do would be to settle on Hardacre until a more suitable owner came her way. Someone with style, who lived in one of the better areas. A suburb with trees was essential. Trees were to the dog's urinary tract what fresh air was to their owners. To have to resort to telegraph poles, as she was doing now, was like being 'out bush'. This was all very well for a while, but it would not do. She'd never been one for roughing it.

Hardacre was showing that grim fair mindedness she'd noticed in all the less successful authors. She held on firmly to the leash, allowed a few seconds for sniffing, then moved on regardless. She was the sort of owner you take to obedience schools, and dump at the first opportunity.

Basically, she would have to nab an author who lived in Point Piper. Or, as there probably weren't any, resign herself to a philistine. Of course they might not favour the blue heeler as a breed, but she could win them over by exaggerated devotion, and snarling at their unwanted callers. She would have to cut down on food intake in the first few months. Once established, she could pork out on left-over bagels and lamb's fry dumplings. For she would have to be careful not to lob into a thin place, where her owners dined on nouvelle cuisine. A good Jewish family would be nice, with a heated swimming pool, babushka, and lots of unwanted callers. The laundry where she would be forced to sleep at first would be centrally heated. Otherwise, she wasn't fussy. The main thing was to dump Hardacre at the first opportunity, she who. . . . Take your hands off me, stroking my ears and speaking in that saccharin and gravel voice. I won't be patronised. Nor will I cope with you, especially if you read your writing aloud at night. It'll be difficult not to hear it, even if I'm busy scratching. Authors, notably Hardacre, were more nuisance value than fleas, more nuisance value and far more lonesome.

'It's difficult to know what to do,' Hardacre sighed, 'when you're so unprepossessing, Delph. There is a gleam in your eyes I don't like. Not unlike a critic on opening night.'

It was a risk, acknowledged Hardacre, that this dog might one day come for the throat. Her coat was the colour of dreams. One night her half moon claws might scald scimitars into the skin. I fear she will avenge me. Yet how can I strike in advance, have someone I know to be human, put down. I would then be a murderer. And worse still, would be unable to confess to the crime. 'Delph, I thought change brought liberation. Tell me why this unreality has become so real. Is your blue coat dusted with nebulae as universal as it looks. Don't growl. I wish to take no advantage of the situation. I promise to look after you, only please Delph don't open my veins when the moon goes behind a cloud at night. You see I want to live in order to finish my masterpiece. Not Weenie's, but something independent, of my own. I will need supreme concentration. The search for truth will make me a slave. Me and my paradox will live holed up like outlaws. I must draw down the blind.

'You see Delph,' Hardacre explained on the long walk back, 'it's not the sort of thing you'd like. The author sits at the dinner table and is rather opinionated, has no ease of gesture, or the air of dismissal you used to admire. Lapses in taste are countless.

'The central character is someone who won't take the human condition lying down. He sees the boredom and futility of it all, but because he is black, he is excluded from "the club". Ironically, this makes life more exotic, appetising for him. The whites don't realise how they titillate the outcast, give life meaning for him.

'His mind is full of being "one of them", the hated sinners who parade their emptiness. He is grateful his eyes are not like their's—eyes as vacant as the footprints of departed souls. In his waking hours he gives thanks, in his dreams he conjures their world of sweetmeats, super schemes and ski lodges. He asks the elders for advice about his dirty dreams, and they say it's all part of growing up and nothing to be ashamed of.

'He plays the music of the bush when he is alone. It is a music of silences and sudden strumming not always harmonic. He takes his guitar from town to town. He blesses the yokels giving off their ignorance as pungent as piss as he walks past. He drives his truck, and each town seems to canter up to him like an idiot child. He leans out for directions in order to make them feel important. When he gets out he walks under the fairy lights and bunting to read the rodeo notices. He pulls his belt in a notch as he passes the police station. And all the time he wonders what it must be like to be so singlemindedly bored. For whites were like the railway tracks which in the past they'd laid down their lives for. He feared them, wondered at them, was bored by them and felt shame for them now they were superseded by aviation. For since aviation it seemed they'd been exposed. The dream of flight was the last dream killed, and there was nothing left for them anymore.

'So that's what it's all about, Delph. Not your cup of tea, or tin of Pal, I should imagine. You needn't yawn. You know in some ways I think you're equally hateful as a heeler, still bearing a glow of complacent malice. But now of course, I can't prove your culpability, which makes things rather awkward. People will expect me to pat you, fondle and make a fuss of you. Will I be able to call you off when you lay siege?

'Zounds hound, I respect your right to remain a bitch. But I confirm that that's the last time I pat you. I need two hands for typing. Your teeth have left awesome prints.

'There is a question I still want to ask, and I hope it's not too personal. Has your sexual appetite become more or less voracious? For, when I think back, you who dined on delay and author torture, seemed so washed out. Was that the result of a steamy love life?

Or did you lay yourself waste between the sheets, all passive and white and clean like a page. What kind of imposition took place? Words and signs you could not hope to understand. Did you enjoy playing fat lamb outside the slaughterhouse?

'I don't think I'm making myself understood. Was it naivete or masochism that so enhanced your book dealership—the chance of making something good, bad, or something bad, worse? For your sake I hope the latter. Do you still crave a good Galliano, or will a puddle or rainwater suffice?

'Delph, I came into your office a measly one. You treated me as if I were no more than a carpet tack come loose. I had a soul full of passion and a mind full of ideas. You bundled me up like dirty laundry. I, as we all do, Delph, try not to bear grudges. You can stop flattening your ears and looking ominous. I can lecture you now all I like. Perhaps that's your punishment. Hardacre harangue from here to the great boarding kennels in the sky. I want to laugh. Yet there is bitterness still to be purged. Your responsibility was great. I was as vulnerable as a snail sans shell. You stepped on me. Drove your advantage home.

'By the time the third book was written, I began to wonder why you were the way you were. Did laziness, prevarication and indifference subsidise masochistic endeavours between the sheets? Do I admonish too harshly? I hope so, for I'm growing impatient. I feel that I must protect my masterpiece from you and your kind. It is not mere egotism which drives me, but a desire for peace. I do, mark do, crave peace.

'Anyway, let's return to those early days when I came all four-footed and friendly into your office. When I showed my soul, my doubts and indecisions, you played judge and chose to condemn me. You sent my soul away for a long term of imprisonment, encouraging me to write more second rate sagas which were as you said "such an invaluable apprenticeship for a new writer". I became your cheap labour, and it became hard labour.

'At last I have broken free. Delph, you know you may be a good looking dog, but you walk like a thug. After "Guitar", I will take no more typescripts to Weenie. From now on, Val and Dan will be proud of their daughter, the writer.'

An ambulance sped past. Delph howled in unison with its siren. She froze as passersby seemed to be laughing, then hung her head with renewed resignation. All this, and Malabar Road. Trouble never came in half measures. She consoled herself with the knowledge of increased capabilities. Her body felt so strong. Aerobics had never left her feeling this good. Her muscles twanged like the strings of a perfectly tuned guitar. She could leap and climb in ways undreamed of; up the scales of major cliffs, down the inclines of minor valleys, crotchety hills, quavering rocks on minimalistic rock platforms. She'd always distrusted the life of the spirit, and she was receiving her reward—a rattling good tune as her collar jangled, an owner soon to go plash in a sea of unwanted owners, and jaws as secure as Long Bay itself.

Hardacre limped sore-footed up the stairs of the flats. Delph bounded up like a schoolboy to a peep show. There was still the ending of 'Black Guitar' to be considered. Best to sort it out in the bath, which was always an understanding friend, soothing and consultative.

Endings were tricky. There was the built-in disappointment of a relationship over. The stronger the writing, the more discontent the reader when all was finished. An ending had to be handled with the embarassment of someone walking out. The writer had to sneak away like the reader's disappointing protege.

What if her character were to throw himself under a train in order to derail it, the only surviving object being a guitar with a broken string. That was unacceptably maudlin. She could conceivably invoke the Pied Piper, her musician leading a group of whites out into the desert where they become helpless as children, stranded on a sacred site, sizzling like steaks on the open fire of Ayers Rock.

Kitsch. For a writer the finishing line was a stage death that did not have the advantage of brevity. There was time to dress for the false funeral, and time to attend. It was a well worn joke, and rather cheap. Yet even she would've felt cheated if there was no send off at all.

Hardacre sank into the liquid depths of her bath. Delph looked on with distant repugnance. She was dreaming of dinner, of fillet steak cut into cosy cubes — meat that melted like ice cubes in new cocktails. Pal indeed. It was fresh meat, or bust.

'I've got the ending, I think,' Hardacre addressed the bathroom tiles. 'Switch off Delph. . . . I'll have him singing at a country and western festival in Tamworth. He'll sing better than anybody, better than he dreamed of singing the night before. Even the most racist whites will stand up and cheer, patting themselves on the back for their tolerance, unable to resist the beauty of new chords.

'Then his song will slowly change. It'll become penetrating, strident, a sharp stone entering their souls. He'll be singing them to death. He will enter their white dreams, road wagons, boring fanged infants, barbeques, unpaid bills, overfed roof racks, tired women, he will fill the angry parsimony of suburban life with meaning. His song will lead them to their cultural grave, until reparation is made. He will take their living death in his hands and show it to them, quivering like the heart of a helpless animal. Not without compassion he will hold that beating organ to the silent crowd.

HARDACRE ACCEPTED with considerable compliance the success of 'Black Guitar'. It was in every bookshop in Sydney and Melbourne. The critics hailed it as a 'minor masterpiece', fighting to heap qualified praise on the book.

'A critic, Delph, is a failed publisher.' Hardacre was nonetheless pleased with her success. 'If they'd been lavish on this one, they would've sent me into scathing coventry on the next. God save their precarious souls, these cutpurses of the literary world who steal a quick advantage or two, only to spend their paltry gains without enthusiasm. Underpaid, seasonal workers for the most part, they prey on the poor, like themselves. Not all of them, of course. I believe there is some honour among thieves. There are those who act from necessity, who believe in public benefit, at least for a while. I don't know Delph, they say such stupid things. Yet their absurd chatter makes me feel less alone. Look at this: "She uses the idiom of the Australian landscape, without really speaking a coherent language. She fossicks for images without due regard for their value. Her characters dissolve on the page like light in a mine shaft. The language has bushman's sinews, but not the free flowing naturalness to go with it. The Hardacre bushman uses his portaloo. Nevertheless for all its artifice, holding back, and lack of delineation, the novel is worth reading. In fact, it is the most honest to date I've read." There you are Delph. What am I supposed to make of this farcical form of free advertising? No need to bark, it was a rhetorical question. Anyway the book is selling like cakes at a school fete.

'I can take Val and Dan on a holiday now. You know what I'm going to do first? I'm going to hire a Rolls to take them across the Harbour Bridge, to pretty spots. At Clifton Gardens we'll hold a ritual burning of the balaclava. I think I can get them into a better rest home in Hunters Hill. Otherwise, they can come and live with us in the Blue Mountains. Do you realise that "Black Guitar" is breaking records for fiction in this country. Selling heaps, absolute heaps. No need to growl, Delph. You'll like the mountains. You've got to learn to control your temper. I thought you'd be glad to leave Malabar Road, even if you're top dog here.

'Look at all my letters. They have to hold them at the post office for me! I just won't open any that have "Forget-Me-Not" on the back. I've heard their warehouse is full of the twin tome, soon to be emptied into the pulping truck. If you keep snarling, you'll go with them Delph.'

Hardacre began opening her mail. Readers were the people she most feared. They stood between a writer and a successive, more objective audience, generation, post-holocaustal wilderness. They were guardians of the word until it reached maturity, some ill defined year. How easy it was for them to abuse their trust. They vote secretly, and what they tell their friends is often a different story from that which is in their hearts.

She read some of the letters aloud to Delph who, when she heard the bad ones, rolled over onto her back and made joyous pedalling movements. 'A little loyalty, please,' reproached the writer. 'This man wants to be my marlin. The other gent on the floor says he knows I don't mean all the things I say. It's strange to have so many letters. It's like I've been away for a thousand years.

'Mail is the best and worst thing about a homecoming. Through the door — no robberies — all is well. But I must now shoulder a new round of responsibilities. Don't scowl, Delph. You can't really resent me. I'm not a hugely successful US bestseller, just second choice for a literary lunch, that's all.

'Val and Dan will be so thrilled when I take them out in the Rolls. They'll bring a picnic lunch in tupperware, and I'll have to persuade them to eat at somewhere exclusive. Delph, are you clearing your throat, or trying to throw up? Perhaps you're developing kennel cough. Don't worry, I'll give you the best care money can buy. Once, I wouldn't have been able to afford it. Am I showing you foolhardy consideration? You know you shouldn't have killed Mrs Bellini's cat. It was a popular cat in the district. Someone will bait you. It's not as safe as you think. I really expect better of you Delph. For I know there is some humanity left. You sneak a bit of television from time to time. I've caught you watching "The Days of Our Lives" twice now. So tearing apart the Bellini tom was less excusable than you think.

'They put the poor fellow on a drip, and it cost me a fortune, what with the burial expenses, and promises to Mrs Bellini that I would pay for her next cat to be "done". In short, Delph you have all the characteristics of a sadistic murderer. The postman has had to wear newspapers strapped to his legs since you arrived in the area. Soon everyone will be awake to your illegal existence here in my flat.

'How do you get out? Do you use the downpipe that goes past the balcony? I'm warning you that any more indiscretions will cause the body corporate to call in the dog catcher. If you can imagine a cross between a Gestapo agent and a rat catcher with adenoids, you'll get a fair picture of your enemy. I'm telling you all this in the utmost spirit of frankness, in case you should want to move on. I'll understand completely if you do. We'll probably never get along. You've always been a bully, a well presented "well-heeled" thug. In days gone by, if you'll allow me one more transformation, you would've been the favourite daughter of a middle ranking Visigoth. Big biceps, plaits, and a list of debtors graven into the stone reckoning of your ken. Delph, you would've slain them at their midnight feasts, shared the bloody cup with discreet lips — full of a sense of your own worth. In secret you would harbour the anger of the clerk, the masochism of the executioner who carries out the orders when someone else's blood is rising.

'I don't mind if you go then Delph. We were natural enemies, just as now, nature dictates we be friends. Who knows what bloody and unnatural events could flow from such a freak of fate?

'I'm going out now, to give you time to think things over. There's three days worth of food in your bowl, which equals more lunch than you've ever bought this author. If it's any consolation, I don't like my new publisher either.

'She's not obnoxious like you, but she acts as if she's doing me some kind of favour. If I were selling wool, wheat, or widgets, she'd drive a hard, respectful bargain. Because it's "literature" she thinks she can buy the author with the book. She treats me with patronage and indifference, as if I were a mail order bride. You see Delph, there can be love, and there can be business. There is no grey area in the middle. The little exotic toy from the Philippines soon becomes flesh and blood. It is a recipe for disappointment as illusions disappear. The author stores up each example of her masta's incompetence — pages printed twice, covers that parody the words inside, class consciousness, promotional budgets that would shame a roadside stall owner. She hates you and your cocktails, your marlen and weenies. From this hate a masterpiece grows. Delph, I thank your indifference. It is you and your kind who spawn Hardacres.

'Your serf has decided to free herself. You've got three days supply. There's no use growling like that, rolling your eyes and stamping like a circus pony. I'm going out. I'll see you to the downpipe before I go. I'll thank you not to return. Find yourself a better house. You've been sniffing round this house like Marie Antoinette in her prison. If I knew someone in a better suburb I would introduce you. But an author's life is not a luxurious one.

'At least Delph you've seen it all first hand, because you wouldn't read about it. You understand now how I am confined, living in purdah to preserve my innocence, hoping that one day things might be better.

'The writer, as you can see Delph, must stay a child — discontent because she has been locked up for artistic leanings. She is desperate to disavow the profession that like a demanding parent asks for the highest grades, is push push push at the sidelines.

'So farewell Delph, I know how much you dislike my lifestyle. It is questionable, isn't it that an author lives more on "fulfilment" than money. I suspect that I write while others drink. It is a form of retardation, a social liability that ironically, others envy. Is it their envy which keeps me going? Makes the hump on my back appear more like affectation. I digress, Delph, as you yourself must do. Digress to Double Bay.'

Hardacre made her exit. When Delph was around she was a morass of self justification. She wanted to plan a new novel. A study of misdirected passion in a country where there are many false starts to be made, a country of creek beds drying up, a maze of wrong turnings.

The question to be asked is whether this constitutes a beginning in the nuclear age. A long way from beginner's luck in the lucky country with its lucky European inhabitants. The ancient land is full of apprehension for Europe's babes, left among the bulrushes. The heart of the sage continent quickens, clutching its blue shawl of sky around a wide girth of horizon. And the stars are tired and twinkling, like the eyes of shopkeepers looking down with some satisfaction. Dull planet earth will make a spectacular conflagration when the time is right—the reward of ambition in a cold and lonely firmament. Not entirely to blame. A fire ball is what it takes to light and warm a space in a cold and lonely firmament.

Hardacre paced the streets of Coogee. Her next novel would be apocalyptic. She would look into the future, blame the present, and excavate the past. Hardacre will make love to isolation in order to give birth to a world. And Hardacre (that's me) throws herself and her absurd story at the mercy of readers, craving their indulgence, yet asserting the veracity of each and every word. If you've come this far you've done well. There is only one more thing to relate, and it pertains to my return home. Wretched Delph had indeed departed. But before I could give myself over to grateful libations, I noticed she'd gotten into my library and chewed down to the very binding, all copies of my beloved masterpiece, 'Black Guitar'.